“What d
around here for fun?”

“Fun?” Abby stared at the man across from her desk. Was this his idea of small talk?

“Yeah, you know, fun.” A grin tugged at Mark’s lips. “A diversion that’s entertaining and amusing.”

“I’ve heard the word.”

“Good. So what do people do at night around here?”

“There’s Oak Hill’s annual ice cream social in two weeks. You wouldn’t want to miss that. It’s the highlight of the season. And my church has a pancake breakfast the first Sunday of every month. Things are hopping here.”

Mark smiled. “I can’t wait. Well, have a nice evening.”

He was gone before she could respond. That was fine with Abby.

Then she realized with a start he’d been flirting with her!

But Mark was the enemy. She didn’t intend to have any more cozy chats with the man who held the fate of the newspaper in his hands.

Or did she?

Books by Irene Hannon

Love Inspired

**Home for the Holidays* #6
**A Groom of Her Own* #16
**A Family To Call Her Own* #25
It Had To Be You #58
One Special Christmas #77
The Way Home #112
Never Say Goodbye #175
Crossroads #224
†*The Best Gift* #292
†*Gift from the Heart* #307
†*The Unexpected Gift* #319
All Our Tomorrows #357
The Family Man #366
Rainbow's End #379
‡*From This Day Forward* #419
‡*A Dream To Share #431*

*Vows
†Sisters & Brides
‡Heartland Homecoming

IRENE HANNON

An author of more than twenty-five novels, Irene Hannon is a prolific writer whose books have been honored with both a coveted RITA® Award from Romance Writers of America and a Reviewer's Choice Award from *Romantic Times BOOKreviews*.

A former corporate communications executive with a Fortune 500 company, she now devotes herself to writing full time. Her emotionally gripping books feature hope-filled endings that highlight the tremendous power of love and faith to transform lives.

In her spare time, Irene performs in community musical theater productions and is a church soloist. Cooking, gardening, reading and spending time with family are among her favorite activities. She and her husband make their home in Missouri—a favorite setting for many of her novels!

Irene invites you to visit her Web site at www.irenehannon.com.

A Dream To Share

Irene Hannon

Published by Steeple Hill Books™

STEEPLE HILL BOOKS

ISBN-13: 978-0-373-87467-5
ISBN-10: 0-373-87467-7

A DREAM TO SHARE

This edition published by arrangement with Steeple Hill Books.

www.SteepleHill.com

Printed in U.S.A.

O God, you are my God whom I seek; for you my flesh pines and my soul thirsts like the earth, parched, lifeless and without water.

—*Psalms* 63:1

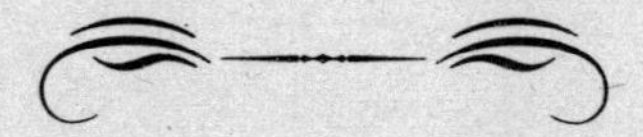

To Melissa Endlich
Thank you for saying "yes" the third time around!

Chapter One

"I know you're dead set against this, Abby. But I don't think we have any choice."

Abby Warner swallowed past the lump in her throat and stared at James Lipic, who sat next to her at the round table in the *Oak Hill Gazette*'s tiny conference room. Twin vertical grooves were etched in the center of the older man's forehead, forming sharp right angles to the flat, resigned line of his lips.

None of the other finance board members looked any happier, she noted, taking a quick survey. Harold Walsh's ruddy face was pinker than usual, his shock of unruly white hair falling into even greater disarray as he jabbed his fingers through it. Vernon Lutrell stared down at the table, giving Abby a good view of the top of his head, where bristly gray hair spiked to attention on either side of a shiny bald runway. To complete the circle, Tony Parisi doodled on a pad of paper in front of him that was blank except for a series of dollar signs.

That's what it all came down to, Abby reflected,

trying in vain to stem the tide of bitterness that washed over her. The almighty dollar. Forget about truth and heritage and independence. Let's just make money.

"There has to be another way." There was a note of desperation in her voice, but Abby didn't care.

"We've tried to come up with other alternatives, Abby, but this is the only viable option." Harold's voice was gentle—but firm.

Much as Abby wanted to vent her anger and frustration on the paper's board, she knew that wouldn't be fair. Bottom line, it was a fiscal issue. Publishing conglomerates were gobbling up smaller papers, making it difficult for independents to survive.

Nor was this a new problem. The fortunes of the weekly *Gazette* had begun to sour fifteen years ago, forcing Abby's father to enlist the aid of three successful local businessmen who were willing to support a free and independent press. Each investor had acquired a fifteen percent share, leaving her father fifty-five percent—a controlling interest.

Then, twelve years ago, he'd had to add a fourth investor in order to keep the paper solvent, tipping the voting power in favor of the board. The members had never sided against him—or her—since she'd taken over ten years ago, after her father's fatal heart attack. Even now, she knew they'd prefer not to press the issue. But bills had to be paid. And the well was fast running dry. She understood their dilemma: they were all good men who wanted to do the right thing, but their backs were against the wall. Just as hers was.

"We're open to suggestions, Abby." Tony spoke

again when the silence lengthened. "If you have any other ideas, we're happy to look into them."

With unsteady fingers, Abby adjusted her bronze-rimmed glasses. As they all knew, the only source of funding on the horizon was Spencer Campbell, founder and CEO of Campbell Publishing, who had expressed interest in acquiring the *Gazette.*

"I wish I did, Tony."

"At the rate we're going, I doubt we can sustain operations for more than six months," Vernon offered as he perused the financial report in front of him.

That was pretty much what Joe Miller, the staff accountant, had told her yesterday when they'd gone over the budget. And there was little Abby could do to bolster the numbers. The operation was already as lean as it could get.

Bottom line, Abby felt like a failure. For more than a hundred years, under the leadership of her family, the *Oak Hill Gazette* had been a trusted voice in the rural counties in Missouri that it served. Her great-grandfather had started the paper in 1904 with little more than a crusading spirit and fifty dollars in his pocket. Her grandfather had won a Pulitzer prize. Her father, too, had held truth and honesty in far higher regard than monetary gain.

Now, under her watch, that sterling legacy would disappear.

"I just can't see selling the paper to some giant publisher who may not even care about journalistic integrity and all the things the *Oak Hill Gazette* has stood for during the past century." Her voice choked on the last word and she dipped her head, blinking to sweep the moisture from her eyes.

"There is another alternative," Harold said when no one else responded.

He didn't need to spell it out. They all knew what he meant: let the paper go belly-up. Liquidate. Close up shop. Abby, too, had thought about that option. And dismissed it, convinced that another way would be found to save the *Gazette.* But they'd run out of time. Selling out or shutting down now had to be considered. Even if both options made her sick to her stomach.

"I'm sorry. It seems I've let everyone down." A tremor ran through her voice, and Abby removed her glasses to massage her forehead.

"It's not your fault," James consoled her. "The good Lord knows you've tried. It's just a sign of the times. The little guy can't compete anymore. At least Campbell Publishing seems to be a reputable outfit. What can it hurt to talk with them?"

He was right, Abby conceded. Agreeing to talk with Spencer Campbell didn't mean they had to accept his terms. If nothing else, it would buy them a little breathing space. And maybe, just maybe, some other solution would present itself.

Besides, Abby knew she owed it to these men to at least consider the offer. They'd all invested a considerable sum in the paper, more out of friendship for her father than because it was a sound business move. They'd lose a lot of money if it folded.

"Okay." She gathered up her notes. "I'll set up a meeting."

The conference broke up, and as Abby headed back to her office she couldn't shake off the specter of doom that hovered over her. Time was running out, and she knew that only a miracle would save the *Oak Hill Gazette.*

So before she turned her attention to reviewing the copy that was waiting on her desk, she took a moment to send a silent plea heavenward.

Please, Lord, grant us that miracle.

Spencer Campbell was not what Abby had expected.

Yes, the patriarch of the publishing conglomerate did look like the photos she'd found of him on the Net. At sixty-eight, he was tall, spare, white-haired and distinguished, with piercing blue eyes and a bearing that commanded respect. And he was just as sharp, astute and insightful as she'd assumed he would be. But instead of the pompous, arrogant manner she'd anticipated from this business tycoon, he was pleasant, personable and down-to-earth.

To her surprise, he also had a hands-on knowledge of the newspaper business. As she'd taken him on a tour of the *Gazette* offices prior to the finance board meeting, she'd been impressed by his intelligent questions. Spencer Campbell was no ivory-tower executive who understood balance sheets and bottom lines but little else. He'd learned the newspaper business from the bottom up.

"I really did live the American dream," he told her with a smile as their tour concluded. "Thanks to a combination of lucky breaks, good-hearted people who were willing to take a chance on me and a lot of help from the Man upstairs."

As she led the way toward the conference room, Abby glanced at him in surprise. "It's not often you hear successful people attribute their accomplishments to God."

"I believe in giving credit where it's due. I couldn't have built the business without a lot of prayer and a lot of guidance."

Although Abby had been prepared to dislike the man who threatened her family legacy, she found it increasingly difficult to maintain her animosity as he spoke to the board about his humble beginnings, provided some history of Campbell Publishing, outlined the conglomerate's growth over the past fifteen years and reviewed the sound—and ethical—operating principles of the company he led.

Instead of an ogre, he came across as a man of integrity, principle and honor. Abby was impressed. And from the expressions on the faces of the board members, she could tell that they were, too.

"When we consider acquisitions, we look for papers that are well-respected, have a solid readership, reflect good editorial direction, maintain the highest standards of journalistic integrity and aren't afraid to tackle tough issues," Spencer told them. "The *Oak Hill Gazette* passed those tests with flying colors. That prompted our call, which led to my visit today. The next step, if both parties agree to move forward, would be an on-site operational and financial audit by one of our staff members. If everything checks out, we'll follow up with an offer."

James folded his hands on the table in front of him. "I think it's only fair to tell you that the main reason we were receptive to your inquiry was because we're having some financial difficulties. Nothing to do with the management of the paper. Abby does an excellent job. But the pressures these days on small businesses of any kind are intense."

"I understand," Spencer responded. "Most independent papers we approach have a similar story. It's a struggle to make ends meet. As a large organization, we bring economies of scale and efficiencies small papers can't attain."

"What about staffing? Do you eliminate jobs after an acquisition?"

At Abby's question, Spencer turned to her. "When we have to," he answered, his blunt honesty surprising her. "However, it appears that the *Gazette* staff is already very lean. I doubt we would eliminate any positions here."

"What about editorial independence?"

"In general, we don't interfere."

"Meaning that sometimes you do?" Abby pressed.

"There have been a few occasions when papers in our organization have become a bit too…opinionated. In general, that doesn't happen under a seasoned editor. That's why we often require that editors remain in their positions for a year or two following the acquisition, to ensure consistent editorial tone."

Abby wasn't sure she liked Spencer's answer. But neither could she argue with it. In any case, his message was clear: if Campbell Publishing acquired the *Gazette,* Abby would be forced to give up the editorial control her father—and his predecessors—had fought with such dedication and diligence to retain.

"Is there anything else you need from us today?" Harold's question interrupted her thoughts.

"No. I'll discuss my visit with my staff in Chicago and get back with you in a few days." A flurry of handshakes followed as Spencer stood, and one by one the four board members left the room.

When only Spencer and Abby remained, he turned to her. "I'd like to thank you for the tour and your hospitality today—in spite of your misgivings." At her startled look, he chuckled. "I've been through enough of these kinds of meetings to pick up the vibes."

Soft color suffused Abby's cheeks. "I'm sorry. This has been difficult for me."

"I'm aware that the paper has been in your family for four generations. It's understandable that you'd want to hold on to it."

Abby found herself responding to the kindness in Spencer's eyes. "That's part of it. But even more than losing a family legacy, I don't want the *Gazette*'s independent voice to be silenced."

"Neither do I."

"But you said you've intervened in editorial decisions on occasion."

"Only when we begin to detect bias. But I don't see that happening here. The coverage is sound and straightforward, and the *Gazette* never confuses reporting and advocacy. I have no reason to think we're going to clash on a philosophical level."

His praise warmed her. And his words reassured her. But they didn't erase her guilt—or her sense of failure that she was letting a century of blood, sweat and tears be washed away. The paper's demise might be inevitable, as James has suggested in the earlier finance board meeting, but she wished it hadn't happened on her watch.

"We'll both have plenty of time to think about this if we decide to take the next step," Spencer continued. He picked up his briefcase and extended his hand. "Thank you for meeting with me today and for the tour. I'll be in touch."

"And I'll talk with the board." She returned his firm grip.

As Spencer exited, Abby closed the door behind him and headed back to her office, disheartened. While no vote had yet been taken, she knew that the finance board had been impressed and would be receptive to an investigation by Campbell Publishing. And intuition told her that Campbell Publishing would choose to proceed, as well.

When she reached her office, Abby sank into her worn leather chair and propped her elbows on the scarred surface of the desk that had belonged to her great-grandfather and which had been used by every editor since. She could no longer pretend that the threat of an acquisition was only a bad dream. She needed to face this. Sticking her head in the sand was a cop-out. Besides, it just wasn't in her nature.

But first she needed to do something even more out of character.

She needed to cry.

Mark Campbell breezed toward the department secretary's desk, juggling a cup of Starbucks coffee in one hand and a bagel in the other. As usual, his dark good looks and impeccable attire—custom-tailored suit, crisp white shirt, elegant silk tie—drew the interested glance of every unattached woman he passed, and a few glances from the attached ones, as well. It was a reaction he had come to not only accept but expect.

"Morning, Lena."

"Morning, Mark." The striking blonde gave him an indulgent smile as she checked her watch. "Must have been some party."

Well aware that he was forty minutes late, he grinned and shrugged. "Too many parties, not enough time."

With a shake of her head, she handed him a stack of messages. "These came in after you left last night and before you arrived this morning. You might want to check the top one first."

Balancing the bagel on top of his coffee cup, he took the slips of paper and scanned the message. "Dad called? What did he want?"

"He didn't say. Just that he wanted to see you as soon as you came in."

"Okay. Thanks."

Once in his office, Mark took a few fortifying gulps of the strong black coffee. It helped clear his head after a night of one too many drinks. As the caffeine began to take effect, he admired the sweeping view of Lake Michigan visible through the wall of windows in his high-rise office. Not an unpleasant way to spend his days if he had to work.

And he did have to, as his father had made clear a few years ago. Accounting wasn't so bad. It didn't thrill him...little did. But he was good at it. And with a Wharton MBA and a CPA under his belt, he certainly had the credentials for the job—if not the interest. At least it was easy. He could breeze through the workday and then head out to enjoy life. As he had last night. There had been plenty of gourmet food, premium alcohol and gorgeous women on the posh party boat. It was a great life. What more could a man want?

Even as he asked the question, the answer echoed in his mind, as it had with increasing frequency—and urgency—over the past few months.

Something.

Frowning, Mark set his coffee cup on the polished surface of his sleek mahogany desk and shoved his hands in the pockets of his slacks, his upbeat mood dissolving. Though he tried not to dwell on that unsettling question—and its unsatisfactory answer—it kept cropping up. Almost anything could trigger it. Like yesterday's call from his younger brother, Rick. A call that had left him feeling almost...envious.

Which was ridiculous. There was nothing about Rick's life he coveted. In fact, Rick had always struggled, while things came easily for Mark. Focused and studious, Rick had earned good grades only after great effort. Mark had aced his classes with minimal exertion.

Then, after they both earned business degrees, their lives had taken different directions. While Mark took his time getting an advanced degree and taking a leisurely tour of Europe, Rick had accepted an accounting job with a small chain of Christian bookstores, gotten married, fathered two children—the second one was still on the way—and settled into a home in the suburbs.

Mark had never understood why Rick had declined their father's offer to join the family business. Yet he seemed happy. He now managed the chain of stores, and though Mark suspected Rick's salary was far less than his, his brother seemed content. Rick's response yesterday to Mark's question about his weekend plans had once again confirmed that.

"We have a Lamaze refresher class on Saturday morning. Then we're going to take Elizabeth to the zoo. We'll probably go out for pizza and rent a video after that. Sunday is church and grass cutting. And we might barbecue. You're welcome to join us. It will just be burgers and brats, though. Nothing fancy."

Mark had only been half listening to Rick's less-than-exciting agenda and, as usual, he'd declined the invitation. "Thanks, but there's a gallery opening I promised to attend Sunday afternoon."

"Your social calendar must be a sight to behold."

"How about you? Don't you ever want to get out and have some fun?" Mark has asked.

"I have fun every day."

Dumbfounded, Mark had needed a couple of seconds to regroup. "You call the nine-to-five routine followed by chores at home fun?"

"I like my job. And what could be better than coming home and sharing a meal with a wife and child who love you? By the way, I saw a face from the past a couple of days ago in one of our bookstores. Mrs. Mitchell. She asked me to give you her regards."

The sudden dull shaft of pain in Mark's gut had caught him off guard, and his grip on the phone had tightened. The mere mention of Mrs. Mitchell had brought back a kaleidoscope of jumbled memories and emotions, the good and the bad woven together in a tangled web. He'd stopped trying to sort through them long ago, instead burying them deep in his heart. Especially the ones about Bobby Mitchell. He didn't want them resurrected now—or ever. The past was over and done.

But if that was true, why should events that had happened more than twenty years ago still have such power to disturb him?

Finding no answer to that question, Mark had ended his conversation with Rick, then tried to put it out of his mind. But it had stayed with him throughout the day and into the evening, despite the many distractions at the party.

It was odd, really. And unsettling. Until recent months, Mark had been just as content with his life as Rick seemed to be. But conversations like the one yesterday with his brother, or watching his father's unwavering passion and energy for Campbell Publishing, or even simple things like observing a family in the park enjoying a picnic or flying a kite, had begun to affect him. Now when he went home to his professionally decorated loft condo, he was no longer impressed by the great view or the hip minimalist furnishings or the trendy address. Instead he was aware of the emptiness. Not just in the rooms but in his life.

Something was missing. That much he knew. The problem was, he had no clue what it was.

The intercom on his desk buzzed, and Mark took a deep breath as he punched the button, trying to dispel the dark mood that had descended on him. "Yes?"

"Your dad's office just called again," Lena reminded him.

"Let them know I'm on my way."

At least a meeting with his dad would get his mind off his melancholy thoughts, Mark told himself as he left his office and strode down the long hallway, his steps silent on the plush dove-gray carpeting. His father's secretary waved him in, and without pausing he crossed the threshold into the spacious executive office of Campbell Publishing.

Spencer was on the phone when he entered but motioned him into a seat across the desk.

"I understand, Charlie. Just do the best you can and keep me informed." Leaning forward, his father set the phone back in its cradle. "Press broke at the printer in Cincinnati. The *Register* may not meet its delivery deadline."

"That's a shame."

Casting a shrewd eye at his son, Spencer eased back in his chair, propped his elbows on the arms and steepled his fingers. He'd mollycoddled his oldest son long enough, hoping and praying that he'd see the light. That one day he'd recognize he was wasting his life and his God-given talents and get his act together. That he'd care about something with a little more substance than what parties he was going to attend this weekend and which interior designer to hire for his condo.

For years his prayers had gone unanswered. But after his visit to Oak Hill a few days ago Spencer had been hit with an inspired idea. One he hoped would work—but one he was sure his son wasn't going to like.

"I have an assignment for you. We're thinking of acquiring a small regional paper in Missouri. I visited there last week. Seems like a good fit."

"Do you want me to check out the books?"

"Among other things."

Mark's eyebrows rose. "Such as…?"

"I need you to do the on-site operational audit, as well. Observe the day-to-day functions of the paper. Get a feel for the place. See how it's run, check out the management style, sit in on editorial meetings." He held out a manila folder. "Here's the background and contact information."

The younger man ignored the folder. "I don't know anything about the operational side of the business."

"You're thirty-four years old, Mark. It's time you learned."

"But it's not my area of expertise."

A few beats of silence ticked by. Then Spencer leaned forward, set the folder in front of Mark and crossed his arms on his desk as he pinned his oldest son with an intent look. "If you want to run this company someday, you need to understand the heart of this business as well as the numbers. That includes getting a few ink stains on your hands—figuratively speaking. I think you could learn a lot from the editor down there."

Abby had impressed Spencer as an intelligent woman with firm principles and a deep passion for her work. Unlike Mark, who'd led a sheltered life, she struck him as a woman who knew what it was to struggle and wasn't afraid to fight for what she believed in. If Mark needed a wake-up call, Abby Warner might be just the one to give it to him.

"Assuming the *Oak Hill Gazette* agrees to an investigation, why don't you plan to leave next Monday?"

The firm set of his father's jaw made Mark wary. "How long do you want me to stay?"

"As long as it takes. Twelve weeks minimum."

Mark shot to his feet, his eyes flashing with anger. "You want me to spend twelve weeks in some Podunk town in the middle of nowhere?"

"At least. And it's in rural Missouri."

"Same difference. Besides, if it's a small operation it shouldn't take that long to do due diligence."

"This is a special case."

"In what way?"

His father's blue eyes turned steely. "You'll just have to trust me on this, Mark."

Raking his hand through his hair, Mark struggled to think of some excuse—*any* excuse—that might save him from banishment to the farm belt. But he couldn't come up with anything he thought his father would buy.

"Give it up, Mark," Spencer said as if reading his mind. "I didn't make this decision lightly. Nor is it negotiable."

Biting back a sharp retort, Mark glared at his father. "I'm not the best person for this job."

"You're the perfect person." The phone rang again, and Spencer reached for the handset. "Check in with me every few days. I want to be kept informed of your progress… Spencer Campbell here."

Their conversation was over. No, Mark corrected. This hadn't been a conversation. It had been an executive order. Picking up the folder, he wandered back to his office in a daze and sank into his leather desk chair. He was being sent to Hicksville, ill equipped for everything except the numbers part of his assignment.

Although he tried to remain angry, Mark didn't succeed. Nothing had much power to evoke—or sustain—emotion in him. Besides, he'd been coasting for years. He supposed his father had a right to expect him to earn his keep. And, as heir apparent, to learn more about the business than how to crunch numbers.

Still, spending three months in the heartland of Missouri seemed pretty extreme. He'd survive, of course. As for learning anything, he suspected the only thing he'd gain would be a greater appreciation for big-city living.

Chapter Two

Dr. Sam Martin strode into his office, took his place behind the solid oak desk he'd inherited from his predecessor and opened Abby's file. After giving it a quick scan, he looked at his patient.

"Everything appears normal, Abby. I assume you're sticking to your diet, exercising, taking your medication?"

"Yes."

"Good. How are you sleeping?"

"Okay." That was stretching the truth. With the *Gazette*'s problems weighing on her mind, she was lucky to manage five or six hours a night. Less since Spencer Campbell had visited the week before.

One of Dr. Martin's brows quirked up, and his next comment confirmed that he hadn't missed the blue shadows under her eyes. "How's the stress level?"

Startled, Abby stared at him. Had the Oak Hill grapevine tipped him off to the paper's financial troubles?

The doctor leaned back and gave her an empathetic look. "I've heard rumors that the *Gazette* is having some problems."

Cara must be his source of information, Abby speculated. Dr. Martin had just reconciled with his estranged wife, who'd moved to town and opened a restaurant at the Oak Hill Inn—and become fast friends with Marge Sullivan, the inn's garrulous owner who knew everything about everybody in town.

"We're having some financial issues," she acknowledged.

"Fatigue and stress aren't good for you, Abby. They'll only exacerbate your condition. I'm sure Dr. Sullivan told you that, as well."

"Yes, he did." But what was she supposed to do? She was the editor. Dealing with problems was part of the job. "I'm working on some options."

"Good. Until things settle down, I'd suggest you increase the frequency of your monitoring."

"Okay."

He closed her file. "I'll see you again in six months. Call in the meantime if you have any problems."

As Abby exited the office and stepped out into the August heat, she slowly exhaled. She hated doctor visits. Hated everything about the disease that had killed her mother at far too young an age and which she'd been diagnosed with just a few months ago.

Still, it could be worse, she tried to console herself as she slid behind the wheel of her car. And it might *get* worse unless she followed her doctors' instructions. The diet, the exercise, the medication—that was all controllable. But Dr. Martin had homed in on the one thing in her life that wasn't: stress. And neither of the options for the *Gazette*'s fate alleviated that.

Lord, help me get through this, she prayed as she drove down Main Street to the Chamber of Commerce meeting. *Give me the courage to face whatever challenges lie ahead.*

Marge Sullivan banged the gavel on the conference table and called the meeting to order. "Has anyone heard from Ali Mahmoud?"

The other Chamber members shook their heads.

"It's not like him to be late," Abby said.

"I know." Marge propped a hand on her ample hip. "Maybe we should call the restaurant and…"

The door opened, cutting her off, and eight heads swiveled toward the black-haired man who entered. His swarthy skin seemed a couple of shades lighter than usual, and there were dark circles under his eyes. Deep creases on his forehead and around his mouth made him look far older than his forty-six years.

"Sorry I'm late." He paused on the threshold, grasping the door frame.

A knot formed in Abby's stomach and she started to rise. "Ali, are you all right?"

"Yes. But the restaurant…that's another story."

"Come and sit down," Marge urged. "Tell us what happened."

As he took his place, Abby poured him a cup of coffee.

"Thanks." He gave her a wan smile and took a sip. "We had a fire just before dawn. In the kitchen."

"How bad is it?" Marge asked, her eyes shadowed with concern.

"Not bad enough to shut us down. But if I hadn't happened to go in extra early today to prepare for a private party…" He shook his head.

"What caused it?" Abby asked.

"Arson."

Shocked silence greeted his response. Such crime was unheard of in Oak Hill.

"But who would do such a thing?" Abby asked when she could find her voice.

"That's what Dale is trying to figure out."

"And he will," Marge declared.

In the year since he'd taken on the sheriff's job Dale Lewis had earned the respect of the entire community. A hometown boy and former L.A. cop, he was sharp, thorough and tough when he had to be. Oak Hill was lucky to have him back, Abby reflected—a sentiment pretty much shared by everyone in town.

"I hope so. Because…well, there was more to it than just a fire."

"What do you mean?" Marge asked.

"Whoever did this spray painted a message on the back door. Something very…unflattering about Allah. Then it said, 'Go back where you came from.'"

An ominous chill ran down Abby's spine. The fire had been a hate crime. Though Abby had read a great deal about such malicious attacks since 9/11, it had never occurred to her that such a despicable crime could come to Oak Hill.

"What did Dale say?" Abby asked.

"That he'd seen a lot of cases like this in L.A. And that it wasn't always easy to track down the perpetrators. But he promised to do his best."

"Well, if there's anything we can do to help, you just let us know," Marge said, before proceeding with the meeting.

An hour later, when the gathering broke up, Abby stopped to speak with Ali. "I can't tell you how sorry I am about your trouble. Hate crimes are bad enough no matter who the victim is, but you were born and raised in the United States. You're as American as I am. Despite what the message said, this *is* where you came from."

"Things like this happened when I lived in Detroit, too. But not on this scale. Just snide comments, pranks, that sort of thing."

"How can people behave that way?"

"Foreigners often meet with difficulties when they try to assimilate into a community. That's just the way things are." His tone was weary and resigned.

"You've been in Oak Hill for five years. And you're not a foreigner."

"I look like one. This kind of thing is hard to fight, Abby. Changing preconceived ideas, softening people's hearts…it's a difficult task."

That was true. Still, prejudice in any form had always rankled Abby. She supposed it was a gene she'd inherited, considering that her grandfather had written bold editorials about race relations in the United States long before the national consciousness had been sensitized to the issue.

All at once an idea began to take shape in her mind. "It may be difficult, but it's not impossible. Sometimes people just need a nudge."

"Or a shove." Ali summoned up a smile and placed his hand on Abby's arm. "In any case, I know I have many friends here who have welcomed me and my family to the community. This is just an aberration." He lowered his hand and checked his watch. "Now I have to run."

"Be careful, Ali."

He acknowledged her comment with a wave, and as he disappeared through the door Abby's expression grew pensive. Maybe she couldn't catch the perpetrator. That was Dale's job. But at least she could do her part to soften a few hearts.

Abby tried to ignore her ringing phone. Her attention was focused on the computer screen in front of her, her mind forming the words more rapidly than she could type them as she composed an editorial about hate crimes. She should have forwarded her phone calls to Molly, the *Gazette*'s administrative assistant/receptionist. But she'd been so fired up when she'd returned from the Chamber meeting that she'd headed straight for her keyboard.

As the phone continued to ring, guilt prickled Abby's conscience. A reporter never let a ringing phone go unanswered. That was a cardinal rule of journalism. Who knew when a hot tip might be coming in?

With an annoyed huff, she reached for the phone without breaking the rhythm of her typing. "*Oak Hill Gazette.* Abby speaking."

"Abby Warner?"

"Yes."

"This is Mark Campbell from Campbell Publishing. I believe you were expecting my call. If you have a few minutes, I'd like to discuss my visit."

That got her attention. And broke the train of thought she'd been trying to hold on to. Aggravated, she swung away from her computer screen and closed her eyes. A dreaded doctor's visit, a hate crime in their town and now this. *Lord, how much do you want me to take in one day?*

"Ms. Warner? Are you still there?" Impatience nipped at the edges of the man's resonant baritone voice.

"Yes. Sorry. I was in the middle of something."

"Would you like to call me back at a more convenient time?"

Yes. Like never, she wanted to say. But the finance board had already agreed to a review by Campbell Publishing. She had to deal with this.

"No. This is fine." She tried to be cordial. But even to her own ears her tone sounded downright arctic.

"Okay. I'd like to begin Monday, unless that's a problem."

From his tone, Mark Campbell didn't seem to be any more enthusiastic about his assignment than she was, Abby realized in surprise.

"That's fine with me."

"I'll make the arrangements, then. Can you recommend a place to stay?"

"The only lodging in town is the Oak Hill Inn. It's a B and B."

"You mean one of those places where you have to share a bathroom down the hall with other guests?"

From his appalled inflection, it was clear that Mark Campbell considered such an arrangement uncivilized—and well beneath him. He'd probably never darkened the door of a B and B in his life. As an heir to a publishing empire, he was no doubt more accustomed to five-star hotels.

"No, the Oak Hill Inn is a bit more progressive than that. Every room has its own bath. They even have running water."

"Fine." The stiffness in his voice told her that her barb had hit home. "Do they have high-speed Internet access?"

She couldn't quite contain her chuckle. "Sorry. This isn't a big city, Mr. Campbell. If you want high-speed in your room, you'll have to stay closer to Rolla."

"How far away is that?"

"Thirty-five miles." When he sighed, she spoke again. "However, you're more than welcome to use the Net at our office."

"I suppose that will have to do. Just give me the contact information for the inn." Once she'd complied, he didn't linger on the phone. "I'll see you on Monday. What time would be good?"

"I'm always here by seven. I'll see you then."

"In the morning?"

"Well, I hardly think we'd be starting work at seven in the evening. Though I'm often here then, too."

"Okay. Fine. I can do seven."

As she hung up, Abby leaned back in her chair, her expression thoughtful. Mark Campbell seemed to be looking forward to this whole process about as much as she was. But that appeared to be about the only thing they had in common. Spencer Campbell's son came across as a snob who was accustomed to a cushy life. He exhibited none of the fire and passion for the business that his father had.

Of course, she really shouldn't jump to conclusions. Maybe he was just having a bad day. As she was.

And she didn't think tomorrow was going to get much better.

Chapter Three

Seven o'clock came and went on Monday morning with no sign of Mark Campbell.

Somehow Abby wasn't surprised. From their brief conversation, he hadn't struck her as a morning person. But she wasn't going to waste time worrying about his tardiness. She had a lot of work to do and she took her job seriously—even if he didn't.

An hour later, when Abby answered her phone, he was on the other end.

"Ms. Warner? Sorry I didn't arrive as scheduled. I, uh, missed my flight last night."

"I hope there wasn't an emergency at home."

"No. It's a...long story." Actually, it wasn't. He'd been at a party Sunday afternoon and lost track of the time—thanks to a gorgeous blonde who'd distracted him. When he'd at last thought to check his watch, he'd known he could never make his flight. But he wasn't about to share that tidbit with Abby Warner. He already had the distinct feeling that she was less than impressed by him.

"In any case, I'm at O'Hare now, and we should be taking off in a few minutes," he continued. "When we land in St. Louis I'll drive directly to your office. That will take a couple of hours, right?"

"Yes."

"Then I should be there no later than one o'clock."

"We'll look forward to seeing you."

I'll just bet, he thought, as he hung up. She sounded about as eager to see him as he was about trading his high-rise penthouse for a backwater B and B.

But maybe it wouldn't be so bad. Maybe the town would be far more progressive and up to date than he expected. It might even offer an interesting diversion or two.

At least he could hope.

Several hours later his hopes were deflated. Oak Hill was worse than he'd thought.

As Mark drove down the town's main street, which was baking in the late-August heat, he scanned the buildings on each side in dismay. It was like a Norman Rockwell slice of Americana—without the charm. A few cars were parked at the curb here and there, but the occupants hadn't chosen to linger in the hundred-degree midday sun. They must have escaped into one of the tired-looking shops that lined the dusty street.

He saw a soda fountain, a feed store, and a bar and grill on one side. His gaze swept ahead. More of the same. No diversions there.

He switched his attention to the other side of the street. The Tivoli Theater looked promising, except the movie—only *one* movie, he realized—had played in Chicago weeks ago. There was also an antique store, a real-estate firm, a law office, a dentist, a bakery, a butcher shop. No Starbucks in sight.

In less than sixty seconds he came to the end of the two-block-long business district. How did people live in a place like this?

Shaking his head, Mark checked the street sign at the intersection. Spruce. This was it. His father had told him that the *Gazette* offices were only a couple of blocks off Main Street.

He turned left and drove past an elementary school, a church, the city hall and a few other businesses tucked in between residential property. No sign of the *Gazette.*

Backtracking, he recrossed Main Street. A small police station, a doctor's office, more houses, a tiny library…and finally the *Gazette.*

Since the newspaper didn't seem to have a parking lot, Mark eased his rental car next to the curb, under the shade of a towering oak tree. He took a couple of minutes to assess the building across the street he would call home during working hours for the next twelve weeks.

Unimposing would be far too generous a description, he decided. The small one-story white structure had a flat roof and was badly in need of a paint job. Two large windows flanked the front door, and the lettering on the *Oak Hill Gazette* sign above the entry was faded.

Mark frowned. Why on earth had this place caught his father's attention? If the condition of the building was any indication, the *Oak Hill Gazette* had seen better days. From a fiscal perspective, it looked like more of a liability than an asset. The books would soon tell the story, and the good news was that it shouldn't take him long to do a financial analysis on an operation this size. If the results were negative, maybe this trip would be shorter than he'd expected. Why linger for twelve weeks if the *Gazette* wasn't a good acquisition?

His spirits lifting, he opened his door—then sucked in a deep breath as the oppressive saunalike heat slammed against his chest. Chicago could get hot, but this was ridiculous! The sooner he was out of here, the better.

Exiting the car, he was glad he'd opted for a jacket and open-necked shirt instead of a suit. But he was still sweltering. A film of sweat had already broken out on his brow. Grabbing his briefcase, he locked the door and made a beeline for the *Gazette.*

The air inside the office was cooler...but not cool enough. An ancient air conditioner was probably struggling to keep up with the blast furnace Missourians called summer. Mark flexed his shoulders, trying without success to convince the back of his shirt to release its uncomfortable grip on his skin.

"May I help you?"

A middle-aged woman came through a door at the back of the small reception area and looked at him over the top of her half glasses. A bit stocky, with streaks of gray in her short black hair, she regarded him warily.

"Yes. I'm Mark Campbell. Ms. Warner is expecting me."

"Have a seat. I'll let her know you're here." She gestured toward some chairs surrounding a low table, then moved toward a desk in the corner and picked up the phone.

Not exactly the warmest welcome he'd ever received, Mark reflected as he strolled toward the seating area. But then, most people didn't like change—the very thing he represented.

He remained standing, staring out the window at the lifeless street, as she spoke in low tones on the phone behind him. A couple of minutes later he heard the door to the inner sanctum open again.

Mark wasn't sure what he'd expected Abby Warner to look like. But when he turned, the petite woman in the doorway didn't even come close to any of his preconceived notions. Slender and fine-boned, she couldn't have been more than five-three or five-four. Her shoulder-length light brown hair, worn straight with a simple part on one side, was touched with appealing glints of copper, and her deep green eyes were fringed by long lashes.

Not that she was his type, of course. He preferred voluptuous blondes.

Still, he couldn't help but notice that her face had character, for want of a better word, and the kind of classic bone structure that would age well.

As Abby watched Mark give her the once-over, her back stiffened. She was almost tempted to point out that he was supposed to be evaluating her business, not her body. But she held her tongue. A lot of good-looking men went through this kind of inspection with every woman they met. And there was no disputing the fact that the Campbell heir was good-looking.

At close to six feet, Mark Campbell was an imposing figure, with broad shoulders and a toned physique—the result of hours in an expensive health club, she guessed. His dark brown hair was cut short, and she'd put his age at midthirties.

As she finished her own survey, she caught the amused glint in the depths of his dark brown eyes. A warm flush crept up her neck. After faulting him for sizing her up, she'd done the same thing. Well, he'd started it. Lifting her chin, she forced herself to move toward him.

"I'm Abby Warner." She held out her hand.

At closer range, Mark was struck by the intriguing flecks of gold in the woman's eyes. And the editor of the *Gazette* seemed even more petite—and fragile—than she had at a distance. As his hand swallowed hers, he was almost afraid to squeeze for fear of breaking something. "Mark Campbell."

"I hope you had a good trip, Mr. Campbell."

"A hot one, anyway. And it's Mark."

"Welcome to August in Missouri." Abby retrieved her hand. "That's why we dress pretty casual here."

He'd noticed. In contrast to his perfectly creased gray trousers, impeccable navy blue jacket and tailored blue-and-white-striped shirt worn open at the neck, she sported khaki slacks and a crisp short-sleeved blouse that made her look more like a college student than the editor of a newspaper. At least from a distance.

But now that she was a whisper away, he wouldn't make that mistake. The fine lines at the corners of her eyes and faint parallel grooves in her brow belonged to a woman who'd known more than her share of fatigue and stress. Concerns about the future of the *Gazette* could be the cause, he reflected. In fact, hadn't his father said something about the paper being a family business? He supposed it was time he reviewed the file that had been passed on to him.

Still, her personal problems weren't his concern, he reminded himself. He was here to analyze the business, not the editor.

"I'll keep the casual dress code in mind in the future," he responded. "I can't say that I'll be sorry to ditch the jacket."

A faint brief smile quirked her lips, vanishing as quickly as frosty breath on a cold day. "Would you like a tour now or would you prefer to settle in and come back a bit later? Or even tomorrow morning?"

"I'm up for a tour if this is a good time."

She nodded, then gestured toward the receptionist. "I'll just stick with first names for now. You've already met Molly. She handles all our administrative work and does double duty as our receptionist. This place would shut down without her."

A pleased flush spread over the woman's cheeks, and she rose as Mark walked over to shake her hand.

"How long have you been here, Molly? Twenty-one years?" Abby prompted.

"Twenty-two."

A warm smile softened the tense lines of Abby's face. The transformation was remarkable, and Mark caught himself staring. Fortunately Abby didn't notice.

"All I know is that you've been here as long as I can remember," Abby continued.

"That's understandable, since you were only ten when I came."

That made Abby thirty-two, Mark calculated, filing away that piece of information. He wasn't sure why.

"In any case, Molly does a great job," Abby noted. "Now let's go back into the newsroom."

It didn't take long to complete the tour. The working space wasn't large. Abby's office and a conference room were the only enclosed areas. The rest of the area was divided into eight cubicles. As they moved from one to the other, he met the three reporters—Jean, Steve and Laura—as well as Marcia in marketing/sales, Jason in photography, Les in circulation and Paul in layout. Though Abby smiled at the staff members and their mutual respect was evident, she seemed to grow more subdued as the tour progressed.

He tried his best to put people at ease, insisting on first names and joking when appropriate, but the apprehension in the office was palpable. Was every operational audit this tense? he wondered. To him, an acquisition had always meant an evaluation of the books, an assessment of the effect on Campbell Publishing's bottom line, done in the plush confines of his office. He'd never factored in the effect on people.

They ended their tour with Joe in accounting.

"How's Cindy doing?" Abby greeted the sandy-haired man who looked to be in his late thirties.

"Okay. We'll know more after the third ultrasound in—" he checked his watch "—two hours."

"The ultrasound is today? Why on earth are you here?" Abby scolded him.

"Well, when the tour got bumped to the afternoon, I figured I should hang around."

"Cindy needs you more." Abby turned to Mark. "Joe's wife is having a complicated pregnancy. You can talk with him later. Bottom line, he's prepared to offer whatever assistance you need. Other than that, he'll stay out of your way and let you do your job."

"I appreciate that. I don't want to disrupt your operation any more than necessary." Mark extended his hand, and Joe shook it.

"Now go," Abby told Joe. "And I'll keep you all in my prayers."

The man gave her a grateful smile. "Thanks."

As Abby led the way back to her office, Mark fell in behind her. Until he examined the books, he couldn't pass any judgments on Abby's financial management. But he'd already gotten a good feel for her people skills, based on her interactions with the staff. He gave her high marks there.

In the thirty seconds it took to reach her office Abby tried in vain to shore up her flagging spirits. Until the tour today, she'd been blind to the building's flaws, much as she'd overlooked the tattered hair, threadbare clothes and patched face of the Raggedy Ann doll she'd loved as a child. The *Gazette* offices had been her home for so long that she'd never realized how shabby they truly were.

But now she saw the facility through Mark's eyes. Eyes that noticed the outdated computers, the worn and frayed spots in the carpet, the ancient metal desks. He wouldn't see the heritage or the passion or the sweat that had gone into creating an award-winning newspaper. He would see just the worn-out physical assets. But there was so much more to the *Gazette* than that. The challenge would be to convince Mark Campbell of that.

Or not—if she wanted to sabotage his investigation, Abby suddenly realized. If she let him focus on the nuts and bolts, the material goods, he might not recommend an acquisition. The *Gazette* would be saved from Campbell Publishing.

Then where would that leave her? The sole remaining option was liquidation. And that would be even harder to swallow.

When they reached her small office, Abby scooted past the edge of the massive desk and took her seat, indicating a chair across from her to Mark.

"That's quite a desk," he commented as he lowered his long frame into the hard-backed chair.

"It was my great-grandfather's." Abby ran her fingers lightly over the scarred surface, her touch almost reverent. "I'm the fourth generation of my family to use it. It always reminds me what went into building this paper and what the *Gazette* stands for."

"This is a family business, then."

Tilting her head, she regarded him with surprise. "Yes. I thought you knew. Your father said he'd given you a background file on the *Gazette*."

Hot color crept up Mark's neck. "He did. I have it with me. I just haven't had a chance to review it. That's on my agenda for tonight."

"I see."

Too much, he suspected, as her perceptive eyes bored

into his. Rarely had he found himself in a situation where he didn't have the upper hand. And he didn't like it. Not one little bit.

Sensing that offense was the best defense, he leaned back and crossed one ankle over his knee with studied casualness. "So tell me something. How do you manage to make stories about church socials and little league baseball games and dances at the VFW hall interesting week after week?"

Abby had to make a concerted effort to keep her mouth from dropping open. Not only had he neglected to review the background file, he hadn't read a single issue of the *Gazette.* The man hadn't done a lick of research on his assignment! Struggling to control her temper, she picked up the phone and punched in a number.

"Molly? Would you pull copies for me from the archives for the last six months?"

Replacing the receiver, she turned her attention back to the man in whose hands the fate of the *Gazette* rested for better or for worse. And she was rapidly coming to the conclusion that it was the latter. "What makes you think that's all we report on?"

An indifferent shrug preceded his verbal response. "What else would you write about?"

"You don't win a Pulitzer prize writing about church socials, Mr. Campbell."

"You won a Pulitzer Prize?" He stared at her.

"My grandfather did. For 'uncommon courage in publishing stories that exposed hazardous working conditions at a quarry operation in rural Missouri, which led to management changes and life-saving improvements.' That's a direct quote from the citation that hangs in the reception area."

So much for his offense.

A knock sounded, and Abby looked at the woman in the doorway. "Come in, Molly. Just put them here. Thank you."

The older woman set a stack of newspapers on Abby's desk, then departed.

"While you're reading the background file, Mr. Campbell, you may want to browse through these, as well. It shouldn't take you long to discover that the *Gazette* is about more than church socials and garden club news."

As Mark eyed the stack, Abby thought back to a conversation she'd had with Spencer Campbell a few days ago, when the older man had asked her to make sure Mark got a thorough grounding in the operational side of the business. Now she understood why. The publishing heir might know numbers, but he didn't have his father's hands-on knowledge of publishing—a deficiency the older man seemed determined to remedy. Whether his son liked it or not. And given Mark's expression right now and his general lack of enthusiasm, she figured it was the latter.

When Mark looked back at Abby, he didn't have a clue how to interpret her enigmatic expression. All he knew for sure was that this assignment was not starting out well. He was supposed to be the one in charge. Instead he felt like a chastised little boy who'd neglected to do his homework. Okay, so maybe he should have looked at the background file before now. And he supposed the remark about church socials might have been out of line. Well, he'd use the evening to get up to speed. Besides, what else was there to do in this tiny backwater town?

With a sudden move, he rose and reached for the papers. "Thanks for the tour."

For a second Abby seemed taken aback by his abruptness. Those big green eyes widened in surprise, and a flash of uncertainty flickered across her face. It was apparent that she didn't like being thrown off balance any more than he did. Good, Mark decided. She needed to understand that two could play this game.

"No problem. I'll see you tomorrow morning. What time should I expect you?"

There was a challenge in her question. And in her eyes. It was obvious she'd already pegged him as a slacker, Mark deduced. He wasn't about to reinforce that opinion.

"About seven o'clock. You did say you get here early, didn't you?" he countered.

"Yes. Seven will be fine. Here's a key to the office, in case you want to put in any extra hours."

Her slight smirk as she handed it over told him he'd walked right into her trap. And as he exited her office, he had the distinct feeling that Abby Warner had won round one.

The thing was, he hadn't realized until too late that he'd even stepped into the ring.

Chapter Four

Abby Warner didn't have a college degree.

Mark stared at her bio in the file his father had given him and reread the information to ensure he hadn't missed something. No, there it was in black and white. She'd left college one semester short of getting her journalism degree.

So how had she managed to put him on the defensive? Him, with his impressive MBA and CPA credentials? Nothing in the file had offered him a clue.

With a resigned sigh, he reached for the paper on top of the imposing stack of back issues, took a fortifying sip of the strong coffee the innkeeper had provided and began to read.

Two hours later and halfway through the stack, he leaned back and massaged the stiff muscles in his neck. His almost-untouched coffee had been pushed, unneeded, to the side as he'd become engrossed in the *Gazette.*

Instead of the garden club news and bingo results he'd expected, he'd found meaty stories on farm subsidies, corruption in city government, the use of inferior materials in the construction of a strip mall, a drug ring at an area high school—the same topics covered by big-city newspapers. And the articles were thoughtful, informative and unbiased. The physical assets of the *Gazette* might be second-rate, but the reporting was first-class.

Now he understood why his father was interested in the paper. And why Abby had been insulted when he'd impugned the *Gazette*'s content earlier in the day.

As he rose to stretch the kinks from his back, a knock sounded. Opening the door, he found his landlady on the other side. Though Marge Sullivan was well past middle age, her gray hair was cut in a trendy style and her hot-pink velour sweatsuit looked as if it had come from a hip teen shop. She was definitely not what he'd expected when he'd pulled up in front of the ornate Victorian house.

"I just wanted to see if you needed anything else before I call it a night," she told him.

Surprised, he automatically lifted his hand to check his watch. Nine-thirty.

"We turn in early here in the sticks." At the twinkle in her eye, his neck grew warm and he jammed the offending hand in his pocket. "So do you have everything you need?" She peeked around him to give the room a discreet inspection.

"Yes, thanks."

Her attention was still on the room behind him, her expression assessing. "Why don't I get rid of some of those froufrou pillows tomorrow? You don't look like the ruffled-pillow type. And I can ditch those turn-of-the-century books and potpourri on the coffee table to give you a little more room to work. The doilies on the chairs can go, too."

"I wouldn't want to put you to any trouble." His hopeful tone, however, belied his words. For a man used to minimalist decor, the frilly Victorian ornamentation was cloying.

She gave a hearty chuckle. "Honey, Victoriana makes me want to throw up. It's way too cluttered for my taste. But that's what folks seem to expect at a historic house like this. I'm a Frank Lloyd Wright fan, myself."

A smile played at the corners of Mark's mouth—the first natural one since his arrival in Oak Hill. "Then how, may I ask, did you end up with this—" he made a vague, sweeping gesture with his hand "—edifice?"

She gave an unladylike snort. "That's a kind word for it. More like a money pit, truth be told. Do you know how much it costs to paint all that gingerbread trim outside? Anyway, to answer your question, I inherited it from an aunt a few years back. I was living in Boston and had hit some hard times. I figured I'd move down here and give this a shot. All in all, it's been a good thing."

"Boston to Oak Hill…that must have been quite a change," he sympathized.

"Life is all about transitions." She gave a philosophical shrug. "In my experience, you can always find something good in them if you have a positive attitude. I came here determined to like it, to become part of the community, and I did. It's a nice town, and the people are the salt of the earth."

She gave the room another sweeping perusal and

wrinkled her nose. "The one thing I haven't reconciled myself to is the decor. Trust me, I'll be happy to de-Victorianize your room as much as possible. I don't mind in the least, since you'll be with me a while. And that reminds me...when would you like breakfast?"

The B and B was a mere five minutes from the *Gazette* office, but he'd still have to eat way too early to expect anyone to fix breakfast. "Since I told the editor I'd be in about seven, I'll just grab a bite at the café on Main Street."

"Don't you worry about that. I'm up with the chickens, anyway. How about six-thirty? I can do sausages and eggs and biscuits, maybe some muffins."

The thought of that much food early in the morning made him queasy. "Really, it's okay. I'm not much of a breakfast eater, anyway."

"Well, I don't eat all that stuff myself, either. But most guests seems to expect it. If you ask me, it's a heart attack on a plate. Let's see...how about a simple omelet and English muffin? Or a whole-wheat waffle with fresh fruit?"

"Either one sounds great."

"I'll surprise you, then. And I'll have you out of here in plenty of time to get to the *Gazette* by seven. But don't you let Abby guilt you into putting in long hours just because she does. That woman works way too hard. Needs a little more fun in her life, if you ask me. I know she's upset about this whole acquisition thing, but to tell the truth, it could be just what the doctor ordered. All that stress is taking a toll on her."

It appeared he'd found an ally in the innkeeper, Mark

realized with relief. That was refreshing after the wary reception he'd gotten from the staff at the *Gazette.* He smiled at her. "It's nice to know I have one friend in town, Ms. Sullivan."

"Call me Marge. And don't be too hard on Abby. It's a big responsibility to be the keeper of four generations of heritage. But she's a reasonable person, and I'm betting that once she reconciles herself to this and gets to know you, she'll give you a fair chance."

As Marge bid him good-night and shut the door, Mark mulled over her last comment. *Would* Abby give him a fair chance? They'd gotten off on the wrong foot, that was for sure. Not that it should matter. His stay in Oak Hill would be brief. He had a job to do and Abby's opinion of him was irrelevant. He shouldn't even care what she thought about him.

But for some odd reason, he did.

After consulting his watch, Mark slipped the balance sheet back into the file and added it the stack on the table in front of him. In his first three and a half days he'd made tremendous progress on the financial audit at the *Gazette.* By tomorrow, when he left to spend the weekend in Chicago, he expected to have a preliminary review completed. There was much detail work that remained to be done, but it wasn't bad for a first week's effort, he thought in satisfaction.

He'd also established a routine. Starting on Tuesday, he'd arrived between seven and seven-thirty each day—which was far less difficult than he'd expected, since he went to bed at ten o'clock every night for lack of anything else to do. He kept his nose to the grindstone throughout the day, clocking out with everyone else—except Abby—at five o'clock.

The evenings had been a little more difficult to fill. He'd asked Marge about a local gym, but since there wasn't one she'd offered to let him use her late uncle's NordicTrack in the basement. That ate up an hour. Then he went to Gus's, the local diner—a place he'd quickly nicknamed Grease's—for dinner. Marge had taken pity on him after a couple of days and offered to fix his evening meal, but her tofu stew and lentil salad wasn't a whole lot more palatable than the fried menu at Gus's. There was a Middle Eastern place, too, but he wasn't a great fan of that type of cuisine. The dining room in the Oak Hill Inn sounded promising—with a Cordon Bleu chef, no less—but it was only open Thursday through Saturday.

After dinner, he'd been at loose ends. His wanderings had taken him by the *Gazette* office on a couple of occasions, and in both instances a light had been burning. Abby had still been there. But he was beginning to think that maybe her long hours weren't so much a reflection of the fact that she was a workaholic as that there wasn't anything else to do in town.

Once back at the B and B for the night, he'd fallen into the habit of catching a little CNN, then reading books from the inn's library. He was already halfway through a two-year-old bestseller that he'd always wanted to read but never managed to squeeze into his busy social schedule. He couldn't wait to get back to Chicago for the weekend.

That was why he'd stayed late today at the newspaper. In order to catch a flight that got him home at a reasonable hour, he needed to leave the *Gazette* by two o'clock tomorrow for the two-hour drive back to St. Louis. He'd worked through lunch and was now wrapping up at—he consulted his watch again—seven-fifteen.

It wasn't that he was trying to impress anyone with his conscientiousness. After all, the rest of the staff had left two hours ago. He and Abby were the sole occupants of the office. And he didn't care what she thought. Putting in a full week just seemed like the right thing to do. Even if he'd never worried about that back in Chicago.

Previously, he'd returned the financial files to Joe for safekeeping. But with the accountant long gone, he'd have to give them to Abby, he realized. And he didn't think she'd be pleased about that intrusion, not after doing her best to avoid him all week.

For a man who was used to women hovering around him, Abby's lack of interest was a new experience. Not that he cared, of course. She wasn't his type.

Exiting the conference room that had become his temporary home, he headed toward Abby's office, his steps soundless on the worn carpeting. As he approached, he could see from her profile that she was focused on her computer screen. She'd pulled her hair back with some kind of scrunchy elastic thing and, to his surprise, she was wearing glasses.

When he drew closer he noted the slight frown of concentration on her brow as she keyed in words. The remains of a snack-pack of peanut-butter crackers and a half-empty mug of tea, the limp bag beside it sitting in a brown stain on a paper towel, lay on the desk. As he watched, she turned slightly to sift through the chaotic jumble of papers next to her monitor. She retrieved one, scanned it, then lay it aside and went back to typing, reminding Mark of a studious schoolgirl.

It took a discreet tap on her door to catch her attention, and she jumped, gasping as one hand fluttered to her chest. "I didn't realize anyone was still here."

"Sorry. I didn't mean to startle you. I stayed late because I have to leave a little early tomorrow to catch my flight to Chicago. Joe's gone, and I figured you'd want to lock up these financial reports." He shifted the files in his arms.

"Oh. Yes, thanks. You can leave them here. I'll put them away when I finish."

She didn't ask how things were going, he noted. In all likelihood, she didn't want to know. He stepped closer and laid the files on her desk. "Dinner?" He nodded to the wrapper on her desk.

"Snack. I'll eat when I get home."

"When will that be?" Now why had he asked her that? Her schedule was none of his concern. Nor were her eating habits.

A flicker of surprise sparked in her green eyes. "I'm not sure. We're losing one of our reporters, and I'm picking up some of the slack."

For some reason, her comment made him feel guilty. As if it was *his* presence causing her to work harder than usual and playing havoc with her eating habits. And it wasn't as if she could afford to lose weight. She was already a bit too thin, in his opinion.

"Well, be sure to eat whenever you get home."

"I don't skip meals," she responded in a careful, measured tone, and he was struck by some emotion in her eyes that he couldn't quite identify. "I'm very conscientious about that. Have a nice evening."

With that, she turned back to the computer.

Feeling dismissed, Mark exited. But instead of being irritated by her curt send-off, he was troubled by that look in her eyes. It had almost been resignation. Or weariness. As if she was constantly being reminded to eat. Was there someone in her life who was on her case about her weight? A husband, perhaps?

That thought jolted him. She used her maiden name, but many married women did. Just because she wasn't his type didn't mean she wasn't someone else's, he mused as he collected his briefcase and headed toward the exit. Maybe he'd make a few discreet inquiries. Motivated by nothing more than idle curiosity, he assured himself.

But that didn't ring quite true. If he didn't care whether she was married, how could he explain the shock he'd experienced when the possibility had occurred to him?

Mark didn't know the answer to that question.

And he wasn't sure he wanted to find it.

Abby typed the last word on the hate-crimes editorial and hit Save. Then she turned her attention to an article about the new, contentious zoning regulation. But it was too late to start such a complicated piece, she decided. Mark's unexpected visit to her office had reminded her it was well past quitting time. He'd been right; she needed to go home and eat. The feature could wait until tomorrow.

Gathering up the files he'd deposited on her desk, she tucked them in her bottom drawer and locked it. She'd been a bit abrupt with him, but his mere presence unnerved her, she reflected, reminding her that forces beyond her control were at work. Besides, he unnerved her in other ways, as well.

In fairness, however, this situation wasn't Mark's fault. He was making a concerted effort to do his job without upsetting the newsroom routine. Plus, instead of slacking off, as she'd expected, he'd been putting in the same hours as everyone else. Joe had had favorable things to say about his financial savvy. Even Molly, who'd looked upon his visit with almost as much trepidation as Abby, had commented that Mark seemed like a pleasant enough fellow.

True, he hadn't done his homework prior to his arrival. But he'd made up for it since. As she'd passed the break room a couple of days ago she'd overheard him complimenting Steve on a story he'd written a few weeks before—meaning he'd read the back issues she'd given him.

None of which made her feel any better about the whole situation. Her opinion of Mark wasn't what counted. The only thing that mattered was Mark's opinion of the *Gazette*. Her fate—and the fate of the newspaper—rested in his hands.

Under different circumstances Abby supposed she might care a little more about what he thought of her personally. Even if she wasn't quite sure of his work ethic or his values, she wasn't immune to his dark good looks. It was always flattering to be noticed by a handsome man. But that was nothing more than wishful thinking. A man like Mark could have his pick of gorgeous women. And *gorgeous* was never a term that would be applied to her, even on her best days.

That's why his comments tonight had surprised her. His concern about her long hours and eating habits had seemed genuine. Then again, perhaps he considered remarks like that small talk. In all likelihood, she'd read far more into it than he'd intended. In fact, she hoped she had.

Because if a man like Mark expressed a more personal interest in her, she'd be forced to discourage him. She'd witnessed the complications and heartache that had plagued her parents' marriage. Watched as her mother battled frustration and depression while her father was consumed by guilt and worry as they'd tried without great success to meld radically different backgrounds.

There was no way she would ever risk stepping onto *that* minefield.

The numbers didn't add up.

Mark cast an annoyed glance at his Rolex. In twenty minutes he needed to be out the door, heading back to St. Louis to catch his flight to Chicago. And he didn't intend to miss it. But something wasn't right.

During the preliminary review he'd completed in his first few days on the job Mark had red-circled a number of slight discrepancies that he intended to follow up on with Joe next week. But they'd been isolated occurrences. Nothing that had caused great concern.

The aberration in payroll entries was different. It was a pattern. A bit random but a pattern nonetheless. It bothered him enough that he wanted some kind of explanation before he left for the weekend.

Rather than go to Joe's cubicle, where they'd have no privacy, he punched in the accountant's extension and asked if the man could join him in the conference room. Two minutes later Joe appeared at the door.

"Sorry to disturb you, but I'm trying to get out of here to catch a flight in St. Louis," Mark explained. "I ran across something I can't quite figure out and I hoped you could shed some light on it."

"Sure." Closing the door, the man moved into the room and took a seat beside Mark.

Mark spread the sheets out in front of Joe. "It appears that there's an irregularity in the payroll entries. I haven't gone into the detail journal yet—that's on my agenda for next week—but this was too troublesome to leave until then. It's always for the same amount—" Mark circled a number on the pad where he'd been doodling "—and it's happened on a number of occasions over the past year. Can you explain it?"

The man shifted in his chair and cleared his throat. When he replied, his tone was cautious. "I'm aware of the discrepancy. But it might be better if you talk with Abby about it."

"Okay." A beat of silence passed as Mark regarded the man. "I can do that if you'd rather not discuss it."

"Look, I'm not trying to be uncooperative. It's just

that...I think she's in a better position to explain the situation. It's nothing illegal. You'll see that when you check the detail journal."

Instead of replying, Mark gathered up the spreadsheets and slipped them into a file. It was obvious that he wasn't going to get much out of the *Gazette*'s accountant. And he didn't want to miss his plane. But now he was more curious than ever. If no impropriety was involved, why was the man uncomfortable?

"I'll stop in and see Abby on my way out."

"Listen, I'm sorry I couldn't be more help with this."

"No problem. You pointed me in the right direction."

As Joe left the room, Mark switched off his computer, double-checked his flight time, then stood and strode toward Abby's office, file in hand. She was on the phone when he appeared at her door, but she motioned him in.

"Okay. Thanks, Dale. Talk to you soon." Abby replaced the receiver and looked up at Mark. "Heading out?"

"In a few minutes. But I found something a bit odd in the books, and when I asked Joe about it he referred me to you."

"What is it?"

Mark withdrew the spreadsheets from the file and pointed out the payroll entries. "There's a discrepancy of exactly the same amount on these particular weeks."

After a quick glance at the reports, Abby looked back at Mark. "Have you checked the detail journal?"

"Not yet. That's on the agenda for next week."

She could stall, but it would be a useless delay tactic, Abby decided. She and Joe had figured Mark would uncover the inconsistency at some point, but she'd hoped he wouldn't pursue it since it helped—rather than hurt—the *Gazette.* Instead he'd homed in on it faster than either had anticipated. And it was clear he wasn't going to let it pass. Since she'd have to clarify it sooner or later, there was no sense delaying the inevitable.

"There's a very simple explanation. The *Gazette* often operates on a razor-thin margin. If you haven't already discovered that, you will when you examine the detail journal. In the weeks you've highlighted, our operating funds were so low that some expenses would have gone unpaid. To help us through the crunch, I instructed Joe not to issue me a paycheck those weeks. That accounts for the discrepancy you discovered."

A full five seconds of silence ticked by. "Let me get this straight. You funneled your paycheck back into operating expenses?"

"Look, I know it's unconventional, but it's not illegal." Mark was looking at her as if she had three heads, and a hot flush began to creep up her neck. "The paper needed the money more than I did at certain points. I just trusted that the Lord would see me through, and He did."

For several moments Mark stared at the woman sitting behind the scarred desk that represented her family legacy. A legacy she'd worked hard to protect—even to the point of denying herself living expenses. Mark tried to think of one such example of selflessness and of faith in his circle of friends and came up empty.

But he did have some examples closer to home. His

brother, who'd bypassed a high salary at Campbell Publishing for a far-lesser-paying job managing a Christian bookstore chain. And his father, who'd gambled everything to launch his company because he'd passionately believed in his dream and was willing to put his trust in the Lord.

Bobby Mitchell came to mind, too, for the second time in the past couple of weeks. His friend had given up the immediate pleasures that might have been afforded by his allowance and funneled almost every penny into his passion—his space fund, earmarked for a trip to space camp at the U.S. Space & Rocket Center. And up to the end he—like Abby—had believed that God was by his side.

His estimation of the woman across from him edged up another notch.

He looked again at the figure he'd circled on the paper he'd put in front of Abby, and all at once the amount registered, disconcerting him further. That was her weekly salary, he realized. And it was less than what they paid the receptionist at Campbell Publishing! Was this an indication of the salaries in general at the *Gazette?* But no. He'd seen the salary budget total. He knew how many people worked there. He could do the division. Other staff members were making more than Abby.

This was getting more confusing by the minute.

"Okay, let's back up. I've seen the salary budget and this isn't adding up. Why is yours so low? You're the managing editor."

Her flush deepened. She felt like an ant under a microscope as he loomed over her, so she stood and faced him across the work-worn desk. Even then, he had a distinct height advantage. "I'm not in this for the money. I never have been." Her tone was quiet but resolute. "I lead a simple life and my wants are few. I care a lot about the *Gazette* and I don't mind making a few sacrifices to keep it going."

Shaking his head, Mark raked his fingers through his hair. "I appreciate your dedication, Abby, but it's just a job. You deserve a living wage."

A spark of anger flashed in her eyes. "It's not just a job! I know what's gone into building this paper. The sacrifices, the passion, the determination, the courage. It's important work that makes a difference. We've won lots of awards, and those are great. But look around this office at the letters from readers. Like that one behind you. *That's* what makes this job important."

Now that she'd called them to his attention, the dozen or so framed letters on the walls registered. Turning, he scanned the one over his shoulder, noting in his peripheral vision a photo of a dark-haired minister on a tiny table in the corner. Forcing himself to focus on the letter, he realized that it was a thank-you note of some sort.

"That letter is from a man we featured in a story about prescription drug costs and government assistance. You can do a story like that and just quote statistics. A lot of papers do. But we put a face on the numbers." Abby's voice rang with passion and conviction. "Jon Borcic is seventy-six years old. He was eligible for state assistance with prescriptions, but when his request got bogged down in red tape he went without food to buy his wife medicine. Thanks to that article, the agency cleaned up its act. And people like Jon don't have to go hungry anymore in order to care for the ones they love."

Her voice choked, and she stopped long enough to take a deep breath. "So, no, Mark, this isn't just a job. That's why I do everything I can to keep the paper going. Including passing up a paycheck once in a while."

Once again, Mark found himself speechless in the presence of the petite dynamo across from him. And thinking how unfair it was that Abby had to carry the full weight of such a burden on her slight shoulders. He'd made a few discreet inquiries and he knew she wasn't married. But the minister in the photo he'd just noticed must be important to her. Why didn't he help? His gaze flickered to the framed image.

"My brother. And ministry pays even less than journalism."

As she answered his unspoken question, he shifted his attention back to her. Now he could add mind reading to her many talents.

"But he supports me in other ways," she added.

Prayer, Mark supposed. But a lot of good that did. It didn't buy medicine for a sick wife. Or keep a paper solvent. Or stop a young boy from dying.

His skepticism must have been reflected on his face, because Abby tilted her head and shot him a speculative look. Rather than give her a chance to comment, he tried the offensive maneuver again. It hadn't worked last time, but he didn't have any other brilliant ideas.

"Too bad he didn't go into the family business with you," Mark said.

"He had a different calling. My dad groomed me for the job instead."

"Didn't you ever resent that? What if you'd wanted to do your own thing instead of living up to someone else's expectations?"

Her look of surprise was genuine. "I never thought of doing anything else. I love journalism. I considered it an honor and a trust, being the keeper of a family tradition."

Rattled by his sudden envy of her obvious contentment, Mark checked his watch again. The discussion had wandered far afield from the purpose of his visit, and he had to be out the door in two minutes.

"I need to run." He gathered up the spreadsheets, then slid them back into the file.

"Big weekend plans?"

He didn't miss the slight irony in her tone. His impression of her might be shifting, but he had a feeling that she still thought of him as a lightweight. For some reason, that rankled him. His shoulders stiffened, and when he spoke his voice was terse. "As a matter of fact, yes. I assume you'll be spending the weekend cuddled up with your computer here at the *Gazette?*"

It was a cheap shot, and he regretted it the instant the words left his lips. His remorse intensified when a flash of pain ricocheted across her eyes.

"Hey, look, I'm sorry. That was uncalled for and—"

She cut him off. "Don't worry about it. You'd better go or you'll miss your flight. Have a safe trip."

With that she lifted her phone, punched in a number and turned away.

As Mark headed back to the conference room to retrieve his briefcase and overnight bag, he felt off balance. Why in the world had he been unkind just now? For all he knew, Abby could be involved in a serious relationship. Yet the look on her face suggested that there wasn't anyone special in her life. And that this was a source of sadness for her.

He couldn't take back the words, no matter how sorry he was. Nor was he going to let the incident ruin his weekend. He'd worry about making amends when he got back. For the next two days his social calendar was full, and he intended to enjoy every minute of his weekend in Chicago.

Even if his heart suddenly wasn't in it.

Chapter Five

The liquor was flowing, the caviar was plentiful and a gorgeous blonde was draped on his arm. It was a perfect Saturday night.

So why wasn't he having fun?

Mark didn't have to puzzle over the answer for long. For some reason, he hadn't been able to leave thoughts of Oak Hill behind when he'd left yesterday. Or, to be more accurate, he hadn't been able to leave thoughts of Abby Warner behind.

Even his father had noticed his preoccupation when the two had met that morning for breakfast. After he'd given Spencer a brief progress report on his financial review, the older man had asked about his impression of Abby. Mark had sidestepped the question by saying that he hadn't seen that much of her and quickly directed the conversation back to financial matters.

But he hadn't missed the speculative gleam in his father's eyes.

The blonde tugged on his hand, gave him an inviting

smile and urged him toward the balcony of the condo. Mark complied, eager for a distraction. Besides, the music was too loud inside.

"Pretty view," the lady on his arm cooed as they moved across the terrace toward the railing. Candles flickered on wrought-iron tables, casting a romantic glow over the scene. From the forty-first-floor balcony, the lights of Chicago put on a glamorous, dazzling display, and a cool lake breeze chased away the close air in the condo, which had been redolent with cigar smoke.

"Yeah." Mark drew in a deep, cleansing breath as they reached the railing.

She inched closer, her cloying perfume polluting the fresh air. "A bit chilly, though. But then, it is September as of yesterday."

As her curves brushed against his body, Mark recognized his cue. He was supposed to put his arm around her, tuck her next to his side, make some remark about keeping her warm—and see what happened next.

Any other time, that would have been an appealing prospect. But tonight the notion left a bad taste in his mouth. He was tired of meaningless dates. He couldn't even remember the blonde's name. Nor did he care. All she'd talked about since they'd been introduced was her trip to France, her new Porsche and the emerald ring her parents had given her for her birthday.

When he'd inquired what she did for a living, she'd laughed and said something about playing at PR at her daddy's firm. Then she'd launched into a monologue about her role on the decorations committee for some black-tie gala and the designer gown she was going to wear to the event.

The inane chatter had grated on Mark's nerves, and he'd found himself comparing her to Abby. Maybe Abby didn't have the clothes or the car or the jewelry that his companion enjoyed. But she had qualities this woman couldn't buy with all her—or her father's—money. Depth. Dimension. Intensity. And he suspected she also had more character and integrity in her little finger than this woman had in her whole body.

Abruptly, Mark took a step back. The blonde grasped the railing to steady herself, tottering on her spiked heels.

"Look, I'm sorry to cut out, but it's been a long day and I need to call it a night."

His excuse was lame and they both knew it. It was only eleven-thirty. Though the light was dim, he could tell by the bright spots of color on her cheeks that she wasn't used to rejection.

"Can I get you anything before I go?" His half-hearted attempt to make amends fell flat.

With a look that could flash-freeze a silo full of the Missouri corn he'd passed on his way to the airport, she huffed, stalked past him and reentered the room without a backward glance.

Instead of being disappointed, Mark was relieved. He felt almost as if he'd been saved somehow. From what, he wasn't sure. In any case, he realized he hadn't lied to her after all. It *had* been a long day and he *did* want to call it a night. He knew his friends would comment on his early departure. They were already ribbing him about his sojourn in the boondocks, teasing him about becoming a country bumpkin. This would only add fuel to the fire.

Until now, he'd laughed at their jibes and joined in as they made fun of the unsophisticated hayseeds in the heartland. But the humor in their barbs was starting to wear thin. Maybe because he'd met a few of those "hayseeds" and was more impressed by them than he was by his sophisticated friends.

The throbbing music assaulted his ears as he eased back into the packed room and wove through the noisy crowd to the exit. When the door closed behind him, blessedly muffling the noise inside, he strode to the elevator, wanting to put as much distance between himself and the party as possible.

And as he pressed the button in the elevator and began his descent back to solid ground, he found himself wondering what Abby was doing on this Saturday night.

Abby punched her pillow and squinted at the clock. Midnight. With a frustrated sigh, she flopped onto her back and shoved the sheet aside, brushing damp tendrils of hair off her forehead. Her bedroom was the only room in the house that was air-conditioned—and sparingly, at that. The window unit was old, and she was hoping to coax another season out of it. Even so, she'd left it on all day today, ducking in to cool off between her Saturday chores. The early September heat had been relentless.

But that wasn't the cause of her wakefulness.

Nor, for once, could she blame worries about the *Gazette* for keeping slumber at bay.

Her insomnia was all Mark Campbell's fault.

For some reason, his parting taunt about cuddling up with her computer had stuck with her. Not that she was holding a grudge about it. She'd seen the immediate flash of regret on his face and she'd accepted his apology. No, it was the accuracy of his statement that dogged her. The facts spoke for themselves. On Saturday night, she'd gone to bed at nine-thirty. Her social life was nonexistent.

Mark, on the other hand, was probably with some gorgeous blonde right now at a glamorous party. And for reasons she didn't care to examine, that bothered her.

But what bothered her even more, she realized in surprise, was the restless, discontented look she'd glimpsed in his eyes on the few occasions when they'd spoken in the past week. For all his wealth and position and jet-set life, Mark Campbell didn't seem happy. Though why she should care about his emotional state was beyond her.

Giving up any pretense of trying to sleep, Abby adjusted the pillow behind her and sat up. She needed to switch gears, focus on some other topic. Flipping on the bedside light, she picked up the worn Bible from her nightstand, letting the familiar, comforting weight of it rest in her hands for a few seconds before opening it.

Often during these past difficult months, when confusion and despair and a sense of failure had weighed her down, Abby had turned to scripture for consolation and reassurance. Reading the words of solace never failed to bolster her spirits. And as she skimmed over favorite passages from the gospels, flipping from section to section, they didn't fail her tonight.

"Let not your heart be troubled. Trust in God still, and trust in me."

"Come to me, all you who labor and are burdened, and I will give you rest."

"Ask and it shall be given to you; seek, and you shall find; knock, and it shall be opened to you."

Closing her eyes, Abby let the words resonate in her mind as she composed her own prayer.

Lord, I want to follow Your plan for my life and I always thought I knew what that plan was: to carry on the tradition of truth that's been a hallmark of the Gazette. *You know the sacrifices I've made, including the biggest one of all. In giving all my energy to the paper, there's been none left over to create the kind of home and family I'd love to have.*

I'm not complaining, Lord. We've done good work there. Your work, for more than a hundred years. But it's slipping away from me. If there's a way to save the Gazette, *please help me find it before it's too late. And if that's not Your will, help me figure out what I'm supposed to do with the rest of my life, and give me the courage to trust in Your guidance.*

The prayer helped restore Abby's sense of balance. But peace of mind was still elusive. And as she turned out the light she knew sleep would still be a long time coming.

It was the perfect picture of domestic tranquility. His brother, Rick, was tossing a large red ball back and forth with five-year-old Elizabeth. A very pregnant Allison was setting the table with a red-and-white checked cloth. And the barbecue grill on the cement patio was smoking.

Mark paused at the back corner of the small brick bungalow, propped his shoulder against the wall and jammed his hands in his pockets, suddenly feeling ill at ease. He had no clue what had prompted him to stop by on his way to the airport to catch his flight back to Oak Hill, except that he'd been at loose ends all morning.

After canceling out of a brunch he'd been invited to, he'd gone for a walk along the lake, hoping some fresh air might improve his melancholy mood. But as he'd dodged young families—bending once to pick up a toddler who'd escaped his mother's grip and tumbled at his feet with a toothy grin—he'd felt even more depressed.

For whatever reason, he'd had a sudden urge to visit his brother. It had been months since he'd seen him. Christmas, to be exact. Somehow they'd drifted apart, through no fault of Rick's. His brother called at least once a week, but the chats were brief. Mark was usually distracted and didn't make much effort to talk. Yet all at once he regretted shutting his brother out of his life.

"Mark?"

Straightening, Mark withdrew his hands from his pockets and rubbed his palms on his slacks. His younger sibling's incredulous expression morphed into pleasure. "Mark! Come on back!"

They met halfway. Rick ignored Mark's outstretched hand and clasped him in a bear hug, which Mark awkwardly returned.

"Allison! Look who's here!" Rick called as he released Mark.

Tall and willowy—at least when she wasn't pregnant—Allison stood only two or three inches shorter than Rick's six-foot frame. As usual, she wore her dark hair in a loose chignon—a style left over from her ballet days. Though she didn't dance much anymore, she still took occasional modeling jobs when her schedule permitted. But being a mom always came first—and it showed in Elizabeth. The little girl, now clinging to Rick's leg, was the picture of contentment as she cast a curious eye at Mark, followed by an adoring look at her father.

Rick might not have a whole lot in a material sense, but Mark began to realize what he'd meant during their last phone conversation, when he'd said that nothing was better than coming home and sharing a meal with a wife and child who love you.

"Hello, Mark. What a nice surprise." Allison's smile of welcome was as sincere as Rick's.

Even so, Mark felt the need to apologize for his impulsive visit. "I should have called first. It's not polite to drop in on people."

"We're not people," Rick countered. "We're family. Elizabeth, honey, say hello to your Uncle Mark." He eased the little girl out from behind his leg, but rested his hands on her shoulders with a light, reassuring touch.

She had her mother's dark hair and Rick's blue eyes. It was an arresting combination.

"Hello." Her voice was soft and shy as she issued the kind of reserved greeting bestowed on strangers. And that's what he was to her, Mark realized. She'd seen him at an occasional family gathering, and he'd visited this house a handful of times through the years. But not enough for this little girl to think of him as anything other than a stranger. That, too, saddened him.

Dropping down to her level, he summoned up his most charming smile. "Hello, Elizabeth. I haven't seen you since you were this big." He held his hand eighteen inches above the ground. "But now you're all grown up. Does your dad let you drive his car yet?"

That elicited a giggle, which brought a warm glow to his heart.

"I'm not big enough for that," she told him. "I'm only in preschool."

"Really? I thought you were much older."

He was rewarded with a beaming smile. "Are you going to eat dinner with us? We're having barbecue."

"You'll stay, won't you?" Rick interjected. "It's just burgers, but we can throw a couple more on the grill."

With one more smile at Elizabeth, Mark rose. "I can't. I was on my way to the airport when I decided to make this impromptu detour. The cab will be back in forty-five minutes."

"Well, we're glad you stopped by. How about some iced tea?" Allison asked.

"Sure. That would be fine. How have you been?"

"Fat." She grinned at him, resting her hand on her tummy. "We're doing fine, but I think this one's going to be a soccer player. He or she is kicking up a storm in there."

"At least it's not much longer, is it?" Mark eyed her girth.

"Too long. Another ten weeks."

Rick draped an arm around his wife's shoulders and gave her a squeeze. "She's a trouper. I'd have wimped out by now."

"That's a fact," she teased, affection softening her eyes. "Rick, why don't you get your brother's drink while Elizabeth and I go put the salad together?"

A few minutes later the two brothers found themselves alone on the patio.

"I didn't mean to chase off the family," Mark said.

Nodding to a chair at the glass-topped table, Rick took the one beside it. "You didn't. I think Allison wanted to give us a few minutes alone. It's not often we have a chance to talk in person."

"I'm the guilty party there." Mark took a swig of his iced tea, then set it on the table.

"You lead a busy life."

"So do you. But at least you make an effort to stay in touch."

Settling back in his chair, Rick scrutinized Mark. "You okay?"

"Yeah. Why?"

"I'm not sure. You just seem…different today, somehow."

Mark *felt* different. But he didn't understand why. Or how to put it into words.

"How's work?" Rick prodded when Mark didn't respond.

"Okay. Dad sent me down to a little town in Missouri to check out a paper he's thinking of acquiring. I'm headed back there later."

"He mentioned something about that when we had breakfast on Thursday. You don't usually do field work, do you?"

"No. And that's not all. He wants me to stay twelve weeks."

"Is that unusual?"

"It is, considering I could wrap up the financial audit in three or four weeks, tops. But he wants me to do an operational audit, too."

"That's a little different for you. What gives?"

"You've got me. Dad says this is a special case."

"In what way?"

"I asked the same thing. He just said I had to trust him."

"Huh." Rick considered Mark's answer while he took another sip of iced tea. "That doesn't sound like Dad. He always gives a straight answer—even when you don't want one." A grin flashed across Rick's face. "Hey, remember when I was eight and you told me there was no Santa Claus? I went right to Dad, hoping he'd set you straight, and instead he gave me the hard truth. I didn't talk to you for a week."

Mark hadn't thought of that incident for years. "Yeah, well, Dad did. He read me the riot act. Said I should have let you hold on to your illusion as long as you could. That it wasn't right to take it away before you were ready to let it go. And to help me remember that lesson, he grounded me for two weeks." That event must have slipped from his memory because it had happened soon after Bobby Mitchell died. That whole time in his life was a black hole.

"Anyway, I'm surprised he isn't being up front with

you about this." Rick puzzled over it for a few seconds. "Anything odd at this paper you're checking out? Maybe he didn't want to prejudice you one way or the other."

"No. It's a pretty straightforward operation. Typical case of a mom-and-pop weekly that can't stay afloat with today's cost pressures. It's a good paper, and seems to be well run. The editor's sharp—although she's not very happy about the whole situation."

"That's to be expected. People don't like change."

"There's more to it than that. The paper was started by her great-grandfather and it's been in her family for four generations."

"Ouch." A flash of sympathy ricocheted across Rick's face. "That would be tough. She probably feels like she's letting the family legacy slip through her fingers."

"Yeah. But if we don't take it over, someone else will. Or it'll go under."

"That bad, huh?"

"I'm just starting my review, but I'd say that conclusion is a pretty safe bet."

The patio door slid open and Allison stuck her head out. "Are you sure we can't convince you to stay for dinner, Mark?"

"No. I don't want to miss my plane."

"Next time, then?"

"Sure. Thanks."

"Well, have a safe trip. I'm going to give Elizabeth her bath. Say goodbye to Uncle Mark, Elizabeth."

The little girl gave him a shy smile. "'Bye."

"Goodbye, Elizabeth."

The door closed and Mark took a final swig of his tea as he looked around Rick's backyard. For some reason, he was reluctant to leave. The lush green grass was shaded with large oak trees, and well-kept gardens in vivid bloom provided a pleasing border. Colorful playground equipment occupied one corner, and an appetizing aroma from the grill made his stomach rumble. He wished he had a spare hour to share a burger with Rick and his family. Or, better yet, had his own family to go home to.

That surprising thought caught him off guard, and when Rick spoke it took him a moment to switch gears.

"I'm glad you stopped by, Mark."

Drawing in a deep breath, he cleared his throat. "Me, too."

"Listen…are you sure everything's okay?" Rick leaned forward and laid a hand on his shoulder, his expression concerned.

"Yeah." With an effort, Mark managed a smile. "I guess I'm not anxious to return to the sticks."

"Is it that bad?"

In truth, it wasn't. Now that Marge had reduced the clutter in his room and he'd established a routine, the assignment wasn't all that unpleasant. Still, something in Oak Hill had thrown him off balance. Why else would he have walked out of a perfectly good party last night, one he would have relished a few weeks ago? Why had he skipped out on the brunch this morning and gone for a solitary walk instead? Why had he paid a spur-of-the-moment visit to his brother? Why did thoughts of Abby Warner keep flitting through his mind?

Abby Warner.

She was the key to all this, Mark realized. From the instant they'd met she'd made him feel as if he didn't measure up. At first he hadn't cared. Then, as he'd learned a little more about her standards—the ones he was being measured against—her opinion of him had begun to matter.

And along the way he'd been forced to acknowledge a painful truth. She couldn't have made him feel inadequate unless he *was* inadequate. The simple fact was that as he'd begun to see himself through her eyes, he hadn't particularly liked the view.

"Earth to Mark. Earth to Mark."

It was a childhood tease and it caught Mark's attention. "Sorry. My mind wandered for a minute."

"I'll say. Where did it go?"

"Oak Hill. I was thinking about the editor at the *Gazette.*"

"From the look on your face, I'm not sure they were good thoughts."

"Abby's…different. I've never met anyone quite like her. Let's just say that she keeps me on my toes."

Tilting his head, Rick regarded his brother with an enigmatic expression. "Is that a bad thing?"

"I don't know."

"Well, you have eleven more weeks to find out, by my calculation."

A horn tooted and Mark rose. "That's my cab. Listen, thanks again for the hospitality."

"Anytime, Mark. And I mean that."

"Yeah. I know. I'll give you a call soon. We didn't even have a chance to talk about your job."

"Yours sounds more interesting at the moment. Especially Abby."

With a forced grin and a wave, Mark headed for the cab. *Interesting* was a good word for Abby, he decided. There were others that came to mind, too. Like admirable. Attractive. Appealing. But he refused to consider them.

Interesting was definitely a whole lot safer.

Chapter Six

The e-mail from Spencer Campbell was waiting when Abby arrived at the office Monday morning. As she read it, her eyebrows rose.

I met with Mark on Saturday and it seems he's made a good start on the financial review. However, I got the distinct impression that he's not yet had much interaction with the staff or involvement in the day-to-day operation of the *Gazette*.

As I mentioned in our phone conversation a few weeks ago, I hope you'll provide him with some practical field experience. This is his first on-site audit, and I'd like him to get a few ink stains on his hands, so to speak. It would also help him better understand the *Gazette*—and assist him in making an informed recommendation.

Mark is aware that I'm expecting more than a financial report from his visit, and I'll remind him of that in a separate e-mail. Please don't hesitate to contact me if any concerns arise.

A wry smile tugged at the corners of Abby's mouth. Mark was going to love this. Especially that "ink stains on his hands" part. She doubted whether his strong, lean fingers had ever done anything more strenuous than lift a tennis racket or hold a drink.

Journalism didn't require manual labor, of course. But it didn't happen in a nice, comfortable penthouse office, either. Nor was it neat and tidy. Or necessarily pleasant. And Mark Campbell didn't strike her as the type who liked to dirty his hands in unpleasantness. Or do anything that caused him discomfort.

This should be very interesting.

As Mark reread the e-mail from his father, his lips settled into a grim line.

After our breakfast Saturday, it occurred to me that while your financial progress seems good at the *Gazette*, your work so far has been confined to numbers. I've asked Abby Warner to assist you with the operational audit by providing you with a more thorough grounding in the business, per our original discussion in my office. Please give her your full cooperation.

Exactly what had his father told Abby? Mark wondered. Nothing good, he suspected. He knew his father was disappointed in him. That he'd expected his oldest son to grow up and start caring about the business and its future. To carry on the family tradition with commitment and passion—as Abby had with the *Gazette.*

The trouble was, he'd never felt the excitement and enthusiasm about this business that she did. Or that his father did. He'd ended up at Campbell Publishing simply because he hadn't felt a passion for anything else.

It wasn't that he lacked appreciation for his father's achievements. In fact, he respected them. Took pride in them, even. He just didn't feel a compelling desire to carry them on.

Had he told his father years ago that he wanted to follow a different path, he suspected the older man would have overlooked his disappointment and supported his son's ambitions. But with Spencer's retirement from the day-to-day operations only a couple of years away, now wasn't the time to tell him he had to find someone else to carry on the tradition.

In truth, Mark supposed he owed it to his dad to give this a shot. To try and summon up some enthusiasm. To go along with whatever Abby deemed appropriate in terms of "grounding." Depending on what she had in mind, of course. There were limits, after all.

Unfortunately, she struck him as the type who would push those limits.

Abby didn't keep him guessing long. When a discreet tap sounded on the conference room door about midmorning, he turned to find her on the threshold.

"Do you have a minute?" The faint blue shadows

beneath her eyes seemed a tinge deeper than usual, he noted, as if she hadn't been sleeping well.

"Sure."

He started to rise, but she waved him back to his seat, half closed the door and joined him at the table. She got right to the point.

"I had an e-mail from your father this morning."

"I did, too."

When he offered nothing more, she continued. "He's asked me to give you a behind-the-scenes look at *Gazette* operations."

Again, Mark remained silent—a technique that had served him well in the business world. It unsettled people, often giving him the upper hand. Especially in situations where he was at a disadvantage—like this one.

But if Abby was flustered, she hid it well. She leveled a direct gaze at him, and when she spoke again her manner was confident and controlled.

"I've decided that the best way to accomplish that is to run you through our standard new-employee orientation. That involves shadowing each staff member for a couple of days. You can start with Molly."

"Molly?"

"Of course. She practically runs the place. I suspect you'll learn more from her than from all the rest of us combined."

"But…she's a receptionist!"

Abby's eyes narrowed at his disparaging tone. "And office administrator."

Another name for secretary. What was he supposed

to learn from a secretary? The next thing he knew, she'd be pairing him up with the janitor.

At his mutinous expression, Abby folded her arms across her chest and leaned back in her chair. "Do you have a problem with my plan?"

Amusement glinted in her eyes, and Mark bit back a retort. Thanks to his dad, she had the upper hand. His best hope of sidestepping this assignment—and the extra days it would entail—was to remain calm and use logic.

Striving to appear unruffled, Mark picked up his Montblanc pen and balanced it in his fingers. "I still have quite a bit of work to do on the books. I'm not sure I need to shadow everyone."

"Who would you leave out?"

"Well, it may not be necessary to spend two days with every reporter." His tone was careful, measured. "And I already work with Joe. I've dealt with Molly, too."

Folding her hands on the table in front of her, Abby spoke in a quiet but firm voice. "Every person on this staff makes a vital contribution. I think it's important for you to spend time with everyone. If you disagree with my plan, I suggest you take it up with your father."

A muscle twitched in Mark's cheek. He was stuck. There was no way he was going to call his father about this. After all, Abby's plan was consistent with what the older man had said to him in his office when he'd given him this assignment. He'd been asked to do an operational audit. To check out the management style, sit in on editorial meetings. To gain an understanding of the heart of the business as well as the numbers.

Considering Abby's plan, he'd need every bit of those twelve weeks his father had allocated to the project, he realized, stifling a resigned sigh.

"We can try it your way," Mark capitulated with a shrug. "But I still need to work on the numbers and…"

A flicker of movement at the door caught Abby's attention, and she turned to find Molly hesitating on the threshold.

"Sorry. I didn't mean to interrupt," the woman apologized.

"No problem," Abby replied. "What's up?"

"I thought you'd want to see this right away." She held up an envelope addressed in block printing. "It came in the mail."

"Thanks." Abby extended her hand, and the woman passed the envelope over before disappearing back through the door. "Sorry, Mark. You were saying…." Even as she spoke, she withdrew a single sheet of paper and scanned it.

"Just that I appreciate your efforts to familiarize me with all aspects of the *Gazette,* but I'm concerned that my focus will be distracted and…" His words trailed off. Abby's complexion had gone pale as she read the paper in her hand, and it was clear that she hadn't heard a word he'd said. He leaned toward her. "What's wrong?"

It took Abby a second to disengage from the vulgar and mildly threatening letter in her hands, sent by a reader who had not appreciated her editorial on hate crimes—and warning her to drop the subject. When she looked up, Mark pinned her with intent brown eyes.

"Nothing. Just a letter from a reader." She refolded the sheet of paper and started to slide it back into the envelope.

"It doesn't look like nothing."

Her hands stilled as she recalled Spencer's request to acquaint his son with all aspects of the newspaper business. This wasn't a pretty one, but perhaps it was important in helping him understand the nature of the work. Slowly she handed over the piece of paper.

Mark didn't release her troubled gaze at once. But when he did, long enough to scan the short, typed message, he understood her reaction. The vitriolic tone of the crude note sent a shock wave rippling through him.

Appalled, he stared at her. "Do you get many of these kinds of letters?"

Lifting one shoulder in a dismissive gesture, Abby reached for the letter, then stood. "It happens. It goes with the territory if you tackle the hard issues."

"But I read that editorial. You were right on the money. How can anyone condone prejudice?"

The whisper of a smile stirred her lips as she regarded him, like the faintest breeze on a still summer day. "I don't know. Perhaps a lot of people don't realize they *are* prejudiced. I'll tell Molly to expect you to stop by and set up a schedule with her."

With that, she turned and disappeared through the door.

Her quick change of subject disconcerted him for an instant, but her parting message wasn't lost on Mark. He, too, had exhibited prejudice when he'd balked at working with other staff members, thinking he was above them. A sense of shame washed over him as he recognized the truth in her comment.

At any other time, he might have resented her for once again pointing out his shortcomings. But now he was distracted by another emotion.

Worry.

It had never occurred to him that Abby's job could be dangerous. Yet once past her initial shock, she hadn't seemed too concerned about the threatening tone of the letter. It was almost as if she'd already put it out of her mind and moved on to the day's next task.

He needed to do the same. The detail journal spread out on the table in front of him required his absolute focus. If Abby wasn't worried about the danger hinted at in that letter, then he shouldn't be, either.

But for some reason, he couldn't get it out of his mind.

By the end of the day Mark had managed to subdue concerns about Abby's disturbing letter. But he hadn't been able to forget the sudden pallor on her cheeks as she'd read it. She might have acted nonchalant about the venomous missive, but for a few seconds it had thrown her off balance. Their paths hadn't crossed for the remainder of the day, and he assumed she was fine. Yet he was reluctant to leave without reassuring himself of that fact. Why, he didn't know. Nor did he allow himself to dwell on that question.

After turning over the books to Joe for safekeeping, he retrieved his briefcase from the conference room and flipped off the light. Abby's office was at the opposite end of the hall from the exit, and he headed that way.

Her back was to him as he drew close, and knocked on the door. Surprise flickered across her face when she turned, and she removed her glasses.

"I wanted to let you know I talked to Molly. I'll be working with her half a day tomorrow."

"Oh. Good. I'm sure you'll find it beneficial."

She looked more like herself, Mark decided. Her color was high—perhaps a little too high. But at least she seemed to have gotten past the initial distress caused by the nasty letter.

There was no reason to linger. She seemed fine. Yet he found himself reluctant to leave. Unlike the blonde on Saturday night, whose self-absorption had quickly turned him off, Abby intrigued him. He'd witnessed her intensity and dedication, her innate kindness to the staff. The more he learned about her, the more he wanted to learn.

There had been a time—in the very recent past, in fact—when he wouldn't have given her a second look. But he was beginning to sense that there were fascinating layers to this disciplined, self-contained woman, and the temptation to discover them was growing stronger.

Propping a shoulder against the door frame, Mark stuck one hand in the pocket of his slacks. "Since it appears I'll be in town a while, what do people do for fun around here?"

"Fun?" Abby stared at him.

"Yeah. You know. Fun." A grin tugged at his lips. "A diversion that's entertaining and amusing."

"I've heard the word."

"Good. For a minute there I was worried. I know you

work late, but everyone else cuts out by five. What do people do at night around here?"

"We sleep. We're country folk, remember? Early to bed, early to rise."

"I must admit I've altered my bedtime since I arrived. But there are still quite a few hours to fill until ten o'clock."

"There's a movie theater on Main Street."

"I saw that film weeks ago."

Folding her arms across her chest, she pretended to give his dilemma serious consideration. "Let's see… there's a bowling alley in Steelville. And there's bingo at the American Legion hall on Friday nights. Then there's Oak Hill's annual ice cream social, which is coming up in two weeks. You wouldn't want to miss that. It's the highlight of the season. And my church has a pancake breakfast on the first Sunday of each month. Things are hopping here."

The teasing twinkle in her eyes stirred the rumble of a chuckle deep in his chest. "I can't wait."

The jarring ring of her phone intruded on their conversation, and Abby picked it up, grateful for the interruption. This new, sociable Mark had thrown her off balance.

Pushing away from the door frame, he smiled. "Have a nice evening."

He was gone before she could respond. And that was fine with Abby. She wasn't good at light, breezy banter. At…flirting.

That's precisely what it had been, she realized with a start. Though she didn't have much experience in that department, it was easy to recognize.

Less easy to identify was Mark's motivation. If there even was one. Someone with his good looks would be used to women fawning all over him, and such conversation was probably as natural as breathing. Since she was the sole eligible woman in the office, he had no one to parley with except her.

As she greeted her caller, Abby accepted that explanation. It was the sensible conclusion. The very notion that the handsome publishing heir might find her attractive was laughable. But as she pulled a pad of paper toward her and began to take notes, she caught herself doodling a heart on the paper.

Appalled, she scratched it out, destroying all evidence of her flight of fancy. She wasn't interested in a romance with Mark. He was the enemy. And she didn't intend to have any more cozy chats with the man who held the fate of the *Gazette* in his hands.

Even if her heart suddenly wished otherwise.

He couldn't take one more night of the NordicTrack.

Though he was grateful to Marge for making the exercise equipment in her basement available, after two weeks Mark had had enough of the dingy, musty cellar. He wanted to exercise outside—even if the mid-September air was still as hot and humid as it had been in August.

On impulse, he pulled into the hardware store on Main Street. He didn't have a whole lot of hope that the small shop would carry sports equipment, but to his surprise it had a few items in stock. Five minutes later, a dusty basketball on the seat beside him, he headed back to the B and B to change into shorts and a T-shirt.

Ten minutes after that, he was shooting baskets on the asphalt lot of a nearby church, where he'd spotted a hoop a few days ago.

Only the thump of vinyl on the pavement and the rattle of the hoop when the ball made contact broke the stillness of the evening. It had been years since he'd shot baskets, and the simple exercise felt good after the fitness routine he was used to following at the upscale health club he frequented in Chicago. It brought back memories of his years on the varsity team in high school. Good memories. On the court he had been able to lose himself in the game. After Bobby died that had been the one place he could find peace.

Bobby Mitchell.

The name had been popping up with disturbing frequency over the past few weeks, Mark mused. And he wasn't sure why. For years he'd kept memories of his friend at bay. In the beginning, it had hurt too much to recall the good times they'd shared, knowing that they were gone forever. But eventually he'd begun to recognize that his reluctance to think about those days was about more than missing his friend. That the end of Bobby's life had marked the end of other things, too—all compounded by his mother's death soon after. Things like childhood dreams. Illusions about forever. Ambition. Faith.

After Bobby and his mother died, Mark had drifted. And he'd been drifting ever since. What was the sense in planning for a tomorrow that could be snatched away with no warning? Instead, he'd chosen to live for the day, adopting a simple philosophy: Enjoy each moment, because you might not have another.

That was in sharp contrast to Abby's philosophy, he reflected as he took a free throw, not at all sure why she'd come to mind. Rather than enjoying each moment, she seemed to believe in making each moment count. He hadn't seen her much since the day she'd received the threatening letter. It seemed as if she was avoiding him. But he had learned quite a lot about her as he'd begun to shadow the staff members.

From Molly, he'd learned about the studious, diligent little girl who used to follow her father around the newsroom after her mother died, spunky and smart and hardworking. He'd learned about the teenage Abby who'd spent every spare minute at the *Gazette* instead of enjoying the normal high school frivolities. He'd learned about Abby the college student, who'd taken heavy class loads and bypassed the campus party scene to come home each weekend and help out at the newspaper. And he'd learned about the day a grieving, shell-shocked Abby had been called home to take over the reins of the paper when a heart attack felled her father.

Joe had his own stories about the *Gazette* editor. Of her kindness and understanding, reflected in her care and concern over his wife's problem pregnancy, and her insistence that Joe put his wife's needs over his work duties. Those stories mirrored the tales of other staff members, whose respect and esteem for their boss on both a personal and professional level was clear.

Even Harvey, the janitor, had good things to say. Abby hadn't suggested that Mark shadow him, as he'd once suspected she might, but he'd run into the man one evening when he'd come back to the office to check his e-mail. As he'd ducked into the conference room, he'd noticed the janitor in Abby's office. Gray-haired and a bit stooped, a vacuum cleaner beside him, he'd been holding a cookie tin in one hand. As Mark had glanced his way, he'd removed his glasses and wiped a sleeve across his eyes.

When Mark returned to the hall, the man had happened to be heading his way. Startled, he'd pulled up short and tucked the tin of cookies close to his chest.

"Sorry." Mark had extended his hand and introduced himself. "I came back to check my e-mail."

The man's grip on the tin had eased, and he'd returned the clasp. "Harvey Thompson. I keep the place clean."'

"A challenging job in a newsroom, I'm sure." Mark had gestured toward the cookie tin. "Looks like a treat of some kind."

A soft warmth had stolen into the man's eyes. "From Abby. Ever since my wife died a few months ago, she's been making me oatmeal cookies, like Mary used to. I mentioned once how much I missed them, and next thing I knew these tins started to appear. She's something else. One of those people who doesn't just read the Good Book but lives it, you know?"

Yeah. He was beginning to.

But if Mark had learned a lot about Abby, he'd also learned a lot about the newspaper business as he'd shadowed the staff members—proving that her orientation plan had been sound.

He'd been to the hot, noisy printing company that had left his ears ringing for hours afterward from the incessant clacking of the presses. He'd attended a rancorous city council meeting, where a verbal disagreement had threatened to erupt into a fight. He'd watched a construction foreman slam a door in their faces when Laura had tried to get a quote for a story on a new, controversial strip mall. He'd been awakened at one in the morning to accompany Jason and Steve to a crime scene.

He'd learned that there was no set schedule in the newspaper business. That the nitty-gritty world of journalism was far removed from the neat, orderly world of numbers that he'd inhabited up until now. And he'd learned that his shadowing assignment was wreaking havoc with his financial review, causing that work to go far slower than he'd planned.

Taking aim, Mark sent the ball in an arc toward the hoop. Instead of the perfect basket he'd envisioned, however, it bounced off the rim, sending him running in a different direction. As he dashed to retrieve it, he lifted his arm and wiped his forehead on the sleeve of his T-shirt. With almost nine weeks remaining in his assignment, he'd have plenty of opportunity to polish his rusty basketball skills, he acknowledged.

Funny. In the beginning the thought of an extended stay in Oak Hill had left him feeling almost physically sick. Now, it didn't bother him at all. He wasn't quite sure why. But he did know one thing.

It had something to do with Abby Warner.

Chapter Seven

Four weeks into his assignment, Mark leaned back in the conference room chair and skimmed through the latest edition of the *Gazette,* sipping his coffee. In a few minutes, he'd turn his attention to the numbers, but there was no rush. For once, he should have a whole, uninterrupted day to focus on his financial review.

On more than one occasion, though, he'd scheduled a day of financial work only to find himself pulled into a situation Abby thought would advance his understanding of the business.

He couldn't fault her judgment, however. He'd always learned from the experience. But the impromptu training sessions were totally disrupting his audit schedule. Today he was hoping for a peaceful, uneventful few hours back in familiar balance-sheet territory.

Those hopes dissolved seconds later when he turned the page in the *Gazette*. As he read the bold headline—*Hate Crime Victim Speaks: "It's Been a Long, Tough Road"*—he almost choked on his coffee.

A quick scan of the story confirmed what the headline suggested. Defying the earlier warning, Abby had tackled the hate-crimes issue head-on. And put herself right in the line of fire.

Clutching the paper in one hand, Mark shoved his chair back and strode down the hall toward Abby's office, his jaw clenched. She saw him coming, and her eyes widened as he approached.

"Do you realize how dangerous this is?" He waved the paper at her as he marched into her office.

"What are you talking about?"

Her genuine confusion only fed his anger. "This." He glared at her as he threw the paper on her desk.

She looked down at the offending story, then back up at him. "You're upset about the story on hate crimes?"

"Yes, I'm upset! What were you thinking?"

"About the need to help people understand the issue. About justice and truth and softening a few hearts."

He planted both hands flat on her desk and leaned toward her. "What about safety? Have you forgotten that letter?"

"Of course I haven't forgotten it. That's one of the reasons I decided to do a two-part story."

"There's more coming?"

"Yes. Didn't you read the article?"

"Not yet. I just skimmed it."

"Well, I hope most of our readers do more than that."

Frustrated, he straightened up and raked his fingers through his hair. "Abby, this could be dangerous. Someone's already not happy. This will incite them even more."

"Are you suggesting that the *Gazette* back down because one reader wasn't happy with an editorial?"

"A reader who threatened you."

"I'm not worried about it, Mark."

Since he was getting nowhere, he changed tactics. "Okay, then what about this guy you featured? Ali Mahmoud? He's already been a victim once. He could be targeted again."

"I realize that. So does he. And he's done a very courageous thing by allowing me to tell his story. I called the sheriff, and he'll be beefing up patrols near Ali's restaurant and his home."

"What about *your* home?"

"I've dealt with these kinds of things before. I'll be careful."

She was looking at him oddly, and Mark forced himself to take a slow, calming breath. She thought he was overreacting. And maybe he was. But even though this might be all in a day's work for Abby, it was way out of his experience. All he knew was that the letter had shocked him. And considering how the color had drained from Abby's face when she'd read it, it had shocked her, too.

"Look, why don't you read the whole article," Abby suggested. "It's a very objective, factual, straightforward piece. No one can take issue with it. And our readers appreciate this kind of coverage."

The placating tone of her voice merely stirred his anger again. But he kept it in check, speaking through gritted teeth. "Okay. Fine. Sorry to bother you. Let's just hope that you're right about your readership—including the letter writer."

Turning on his heel, he exited her office and returned to the conference room, closing the door with more force than necessary.

Abby stared after him, confused by his tirade. She had no idea what had prompted it—unless he was worried about the welfare of the *Gazette*. But that didn't quite ring true. There had been an almost personal element to his anger. As if he was worried about *her*. Abby the person, not Abby the editor.

She had to be wrong, of course. He hardly knew her. And she'd done little to remedy that, avoiding him as much as possible over the past couple of weeks. Yet her instincts told her that her intuition was correct. That Mark had stormed into her office because he cared about her.

That wasn't a good thing, she reminded herself.

But try as she might, she couldn't quell the sudden glow of happiness that warmed her heart.

"Excuse me...could I interrupt you for a minute?"

Distracted, Mark grabbed the basketball and turned toward the voice. A fortyish sandy-haired man, attired in black slacks and an open-necked shirt, was standing across the church parking lot a dozen yards away.

Tucking the ball under his arm, Mark closed the distance between them. At closer range, the man had a pleasant, open face and startling blue eyes.

He held out his hand. "I'm Craig Andrews. The pastor of this church."

As Mark returned the firm clasp, he felt like a kid caught with his hand in the proverbial cookie jar. He supposed he was trespassing—and being called to task for it, even if the lot was deserted on a Monday night. "Mark Campbell. Sorry to intrude. I realize this isn't public property and I didn't mean to—"

"Hey, no problem." The man lifted a hand to cut him off. "I'm glad to see the hoop being put to use."

"Thanks. I'm spending a few weeks here doing some business at the *Gazette* and I'm going stir-crazy in the evenings."

"Abby mentioned your visit."

What else had she mentioned? Mark wondered. He'd hardly seen her since the incident in her office the prior week, when he'd taken her to task for the hate-crimes article. He figured she must be mad at him. Better to steer clear of topics related to Abby.

"I'm used to a regular exercise routine, and the NordicTrack at the Oak Hill Inn wasn't cutting it. I'd rather be outside, anyway. And the hoop was convenient."

"You're very good."

"I played on the varsity team in high school, but I haven't picked up a basketball since then." Mark dismissed the man's praise with a shrug. "I guess it's like riding a bicycle. You never forget the basics."

"I'm hoping I can persuade you to pass some of your knowledge on."

"I'm not sure I understand." Puzzled, Mark eyed the minister.

"Of course not." The man gave a chagrined chuckle. "It would help if I explained, wouldn't it? For the past couple of years, some of the boys in our congregation have been after me to form a basketball team. It took a while, but I finally managed to convince one of our adult members to act as a coach. Even though the season doesn't begin until January, Jim wanted to start working with the boys now, since most of them have zero experience.

"Long story short, after two practices he fell off a ladder at his house and broke his leg. I figured the team would have to disband until he recovered, but now I'm wondering if there might be an alternative. Your appearance seems almost providential."

Mark's confusion changed to wariness. "I'm not a coach. And I'm not into…religion."

"Neither is Jim. A coach, that is. As for religion—that's not a job requirement." The minister smiled. "The thing is, I'm not looking for a pro. Just someone who'll take a genuine interest in helping the boys learn the basics. It's only a couple of nights a week, and a handful of weekend pickup games that Jim organized with some neighboring teams to give the boys a little practice. He should be back on his feet in six to eight weeks, so it's not a long-term commitment. I'd do it myself, but I'm a total klutz when it comes to athletics."

The man's friendly approach made it hard to say no.

"How old are these kids?" Mark asked.

"Thirteen and fourteen. Not the easiest age."

A shadow darkened Mark's eyes. The minister was right. It was a tough time even under the best of circumstances. But for him it had been a nightmare. Even after all these years, his memories from that traumatic period remained painful.

"I can see that you relate to that."

The pastor's words jerked Mark back to reality.

There was kindness and insight in the man's discerning eyes, and for an instant Mark was tempted to share his story with him. It was an urge he didn't understand—and one he wrestled into submission. He never talked about that period in his life. Not to family, not to friends. And he wasn't about to spill his guts to a stranger. The mere fact that he'd even considered doing so astounded him.

"Yeah. I was there once. Long ago." His voice came out gruff—and not quite steady.

If the man noticed Mark's sudden unease, he let it pass. "Disappointments are amplified at that age. Of course, it's not the end of the world if the boys have to postpone things for a couple of months, but they've already been waiting two years to get this team organized. I hate to lose the momentum or the enthusiasm."

A cardinal chirped in a nearby tree, and Mark looked up as the scarlet bird spread its wings and took flight, soaring high against the cobalt blue sky. It wasn't as if he had anything better to do in the evenings, he reflected. He was also growing tired of the weekend commute to Chicago. And even more tired of the restlessness that plagued him once he arrived, as he wandered through the sterile rooms in his condo or forced himself to attend the kind of social events that were rapidly losing their appeal. A few weekends in Oak Hill might be a nice change of pace.

"Okay, Reverend. I'll give it a shot."

"The boys will be thrilled." Smiling, the man held out his hand. Mark took it in a firm grip. "I can't thank you enough for stepping in."

"When do they practice?"

"Tuesday and Thursday, from six to seven. But we can change that if it doesn't work for you."

"No. That's fine. When's the first pickup game?"

"It's scheduled for Saturday, but we might want to cancel since they've had very little practice."

"Why don't we let it stand? We'll have practice tomorrow and Thursday. It won't hurt to give the boys a taste of competition."

"Okay. I'll tell the team to meet you out here tomorrow night. God bless you."

As the man retraced his steps across the parking lot, his parting words echoed in Mark's ears. Aside from his father and Rick—and now Abby—Mark had had little contact with people of faith. Most of his acquaintances scoffed at religion, if they discussed it at all. They preferred to take control of their own lives rather than confer with a higher power or follow a set of moral laws they considered to be stodgy and outdated.

Somehow Mark had fallen into that same pattern—even though he knew that any sense of control was an illusion. He'd learned that at a young age, after the back-to-back losses of two people who meant the world to him. Things just…happened. Good as well as bad. Whether by chance or design, he didn't much care. All he knew was that if God really was up there orchestrating things, He'd fallen down on the job way too often.

Still, he respected people who had faith. Even envied them a little. And he appreciated the good intentions behind the minister's parting blessing. He just didn't put a whole lot of stock in it.

Because experience had taught him that God didn't listen.

Ragtag was a generous description for the eight lanky boys with long, gangly legs who clustered around them as Reverend Andrews made the introductions the next night in the parking lot. Attired in a variety of mismatched outfits, the team members displayed typical adolescent behavior as they attempted to mask their enthusiasm in order to appear cool.

Jim Jackson, their coach, had called Mark at the *Gazette* to fill him in on the practice sessions to date and thank him for stepping in. Based on that conversation, Mark had concluded that the team would need a lot of work. That conclusion was borne out when he ran the boys through a few drills and they spent more time chasing the ball than dribbling, passing or shooting.

Although the practice was exhausting, to his surprise, it was also satisfying. The boys had been eager, interested learners, responding well to instruction and high-fiving each other for improvements and accomplishments. Already Mark had identified a couple of kids who showed special promise. He'd work with them a bit more next session as they prepared for their first practice game.

"Okay, that's it for tonight," Mark called at last, after a quick check of his watch. "Homework awaits."

When his comment was met with groans and grumbles, he grinned and propped his fists on his hips.

"Thursday we'll start with a review of the rules and assign positions for Saturday's game. If you get a chance tomorrow, practice a few of the things we worked on."

As the boys dispersed, Mark dropped to one knee to tie his shoe. When a shadow fell across the pavement in front of him, he looked up to find one of the two boys he'd singled out earlier standing a couple of feet away.

"Hi, Evan. What can I do for you?"

"I know practice is over, but I wondered if you'd show me that spin move again so I can work on it tomorrow."

It didn't surprise him that the boy had focused on that maneuver. Mark had introduced it to the group, but it hadn't taken him long to realize that it was way beyond the sketchy ability of most of the team members. He'd moved on rather than frustrate them. But with his raw talent, Evan might be able to master it.

"Sure." He picked up the ball and rose to demonstrate. "This is a great move to get around a defender in the open court. But you have to protect the ball or it could be stolen from behind you, on your blind side, as you spin."

With a deft move, he demonstrated the maneuver, pivoting on his front foot, then pulling the ball hard and fast around his body to continue the dribble with the opposite hand.

"And you have to be careful not to get your hand under the ball or you'll get a carrying violation," he said, passing the ball to Evan.

The boy tried the spin a few times, with Mark correcting his stance and position, and after a couple of minutes he seemed to grasp the rudiments, even if the execution was shaky.

"Not bad for a first attempt," Mark told him, impressed. "We'll go over it again Thursday if you like."

"Yeah. Thanks." The boy handed the ball back to Mark. "Listen, the guys…we really appreciate this. We were pretty bummed when Mr. Jackson got hurt."

"Glad I could help out. See you Thursday."

As the boy struck off down the street, Mark balanced the ball in one hand and looked after him. He couldn't remember the last time he'd gotten involved in anything that required him to give without expecting some kind of return. Including relationships. Yet he hadn't approached this temporary coaching gig with that attitude. It had just seemed like a good way to fill up his empty evenings. He hadn't expected any kind of payoff.

Much to his surprise, however, there was one—though it wasn't tangible. It was more like a feeling. Of fulfillment, perhaps. As if he'd made a difference somehow.

But even if Mark couldn't quite identify the payoff, he did know one thing.

It felt good.

On Friday afternoon, his thoughts on tomorrow's game, Mark used the flat surface of a table beside the copy machine to tap the sheaf of papers into a neat stack. As Abby and Molly passed by, he gave them a distracted glance.

Then he looked again.

Something was up.

There had been an almost palpable tension in the air

as the women passed by, reflected in the rigid line of Abby's shoulders and Molly's worried expression.

His first impulse was to follow them, but he reined that in. Knowing that his presence at the *Gazette* had the staff on edge, Mark had done his best to keep a low profile. In general, he hadn't stuck his nose into anything that wasn't relevant to his investigation. Last week, when he'd confronted Abby about the hate-crimes article, was the one notable exception. He hadn't made that mistake again, nor did he plan to repeat it during the remainder of his stay.

But there were strange vibes in the air.

In the end, he broke his rule again and followed the women. He found them outside the back door, conversing in low tones.

They looked up in surprise when he joined them. "I saw you walk by, and wondered if there was some kind of a problem."

"We can handle it," Abby dismissed him.

"Fine. Sorry to bother you." Feeling rebuffed, Mark turned to go.

He had his hand on the door when Molly spoke.

"Maybe he's run into this kind of thing before." Mark paused as Molly directed her comment to Abby. "Campbell Publishing is a big outfit."

Shifting his attention to Abby, Mark saw a flash of uncertainty in her eyes—and used it to his advantage. "What kind of thing?"

With a resigned sigh, Abby gestured behind him. "Molly found that a little while ago."

Turning, Mark looked around. A brown corrugated

box, taped closed and addressed to Abby, stood on the ground a few feet away.

Puzzled, he turned back to the women. "What is it?"

"We don't know. But this was on top." Abby handed over a copy of the last issue of the *Gazette,* opened to the hate-crime story, which was circled in red.

Mark's breath caught in his throat. "We need to call the police."

"That's a waste of their time," Abby responded.

"Not if this is a bomb."

Molly gasped and took a quick step back, but Abby's expression was incredulous. "That's crazy!"

"Yeah, it is. But there are a lot of crazy people in this world," Mark countered. "You had a hate crime here, remember?"

"Okay. Fine. I'll call Dale, our sheriff," Abby capitulated.

Without a word, he handed her his cell phone, then took her arm and urged her away from the building. At least it was lunchtime and the place was deserted. "Molly, why don't you lock the front door while we wait for the sheriff?" Mark suggested. "I doubt he's going to want anyone inside until this is resolved."

"Okay."

Molly disappeared around the side of the building, and Abby looked up at Mark as the steady pressure of his arm propelled her away from the back door. "I think you're overreacting."

"Maybe. We'll let the sheriff decide."

When Mark at last released her arm, she tapped in a number on his cell phone, then spoke. "Hey, Dale. It's

Abby. We have a rather interesting situation at the *Gazette.*" While she explained it to the sheriff, telling him about the first note, as well, Mark surveyed the vacant lot behind the building, hoping to spot a clue about who might have left the package. But to his untrained eye nothing looked amiss.

Not that the sheriff would have any better luck, he speculated. In a town the size of Oak Hill, the local cop most likely spent his days writing parking tickets and helping old ladies retrieve cats from trees. His experience with bombs and bomb threats was probably nil.

To his surprise, however, the fit, late-thirtyish sheriff who stepped out of a patrol car a few minutes later was no Barney Fife. He asked a few crisp, pertinent questions, told Abby he'd instructed Molly to remain in front, then started to move in on the suspicious box.

"Hey…shouldn't you bring in an expert or a bomb-sniffing dog or something?" Mark called after him.

The dark-haired man turned, his steel-blue eyes sharp, incisive and sure. "If this was L.A., I'd say yes. But so far my investigation into the arson case leads me to believe it's an amateurish, unsophisticated effort. Almost pranklike. I have no reason to think this is anything more than that. If I feel differently after I look the box over, I'll take appropriate action. Any other questions?"

Mark backed off. "No. I'm sure you know what you're doing."

"Let's hope so." A brief, humorless smile touched the man's lips.

As Dale approached the box, Abby spoke in a

subdued voice. "Dale's an Oak Hill boy, but he was an L.A. cop for ten years before he came home. I think he spent a couple of years on the bomb-and-arson squad there. He's very good, and he doesn't take chances."

They watched in silence as Dale crouched down and scrutinized the box without touching it. Then he leaned over and sniffed. Reaching into his back pocket, he withdrew a pair of latex gloves and a box cutter. After pulling on the gloves, he eased the blade under the clear tape, slit it, then lifted the lid. A few seconds later, he stood, stepped back and motioned for Abby and Mark to join him.

When they were still a couple of feet away, an overpowering stench brought Mark to a dead stop. Abby kept moving. She leaned over the box, peered in, and wrinkled her nose as she stepped back.

"Did you see the note on top?" Dale asked.

"Yes."

Confused, Mark edged closer to read the cryptic note, scrawled in block letters.

THIS IS WHAT I THINK OF YOUR COVERAGE.

"What is that smell?" He made a hasty retreat from the rancid odor.

"Manure," Dale replied. "Like I said—amateurish. I may be able to get some prints from the tape. Hang tight. I'll be back in a minute."

"Manure?" Mark repeated as Dale walked around the side of the building.

"Uh-huh. We're in the country, remember?" Folding her arms over her chest, Abby gave him a stiff smile and transferred her attention back to the box. "I may not like his methods, but I have to admire the clarity of his message."

"How can you joke about this?"

At Mark's sharp tone, Abby's smile evaporated, and her pale face lost even more color.

The sheriff noticed her pallor, as well, when he rejoined them. He stopped beside her and put a hand on her arm. "You okay?"

His gentle inquiry and the concern in his eyes didn't escape Mark's notice.

"I'm fine. Thanks."

"I want you to be careful until we figure out who's doing this. Don't take any chances."

"I won't."

After studying her for another moment, Dale went about his business. By the time he had the offending box secured inside a plastic bag and had hefted it in his arms, his muscles bunching below the sleeves of his short-sleeved shirt, the returning *Gazette* staff had begun wandering back to check out the excitement.

Abby said a perfunctory goodbye to Dale, then focused on reassuring the employees as she ushered them inside. Only when all questions had been answered and concerns addressed did she turn to Mark, who stood some distance away.

"Are you coming back in?"

"In a minute."

Alone in the vacant lot, Mark took a few minutes to process what had transpired. Although the box had turned out to be harmless, he wasn't sorry he'd insisted that Abby call the sheriff. There had been no sense taking a chance. Nor was he convinced that the perpetrator wouldn't send another message, perhaps with more serious repercussions. That weighed on his mind.

The easy familiarity and affection between Dale and Abby did, too. What kind of relationship did they have? He doubted it was a romantic one. Not after Abby's reaction to his unkind jibe about cuddling up with her computer. He'd had the distinct impression that there wasn't a man in her life.

Then again, what did he know? In light of the evidence he'd seen today, it was possible he'd misinterpreted her reaction to his remark. Anyone could see there was a connection between her and the sheriff. And that was a good thing, he told himself. He should be happy Abby had someone in her life.

Yet for some reason he wasn't. In fact, the very thought that she might be involved with Dale—or with anyone, for that matter—bothered him. A lot. It was almost as if he was…jealous. He didn't have much experience with that emotion, however. Most of the women he'd dated had meant little to him. In almost every case he'd been the one to end the relationship when he sensed that the woman was getting too serious.

Still, he had a feeling that the resentment and possessiveness and suspicion now weaving a tangled web in his mind fit the classic description of jealousy.

That made no sense, though. He couldn't be jealous of Dale. That would imply he cared for Abby on a personal level.

Mark reentered the building and returned to his financial review, determined not to let his troubling thoughts ruin his concentration. He'd always been good at putting personal issues aside and concentrating on the job at hand. It was a skill that had never failed him.

But he soon discovered there was a first time for everything.

Chapter Eight

The *Gazette* offices were stifling.

As Mark stepped into the foyer Saturday morning, a film of sweat broke out on his forehead. Abby must turn the air off on weekends to save on the electric bill, he speculated. Good thing he was dressed for the pickup game, in shorts and a T-shirt. Still, he didn't intend to linger. As soon as he retrieved his errant cell phone, he was out of here.

He'd pocketed the phone and was heading toward the front door when he heard the copy machine kick into gear. Startled, he came to an abrupt stop, then cautiously retraced his steps. When the machine came into view, he somehow wasn't surprised to find Abby standing in front of it, her back to him. The woman seemed to live at the *Gazette*.

What did surprise him was her clothes. Instead of her customary slacks and crisp blouse, she wore running shorts and a tank top that hinted at her curves. Mark couldn't help noticing that she was soft and rounded in all the right places despite her lean physique. When she reached up to return a three-hole punch to an overhead shelf, her top crept up, revealing her trim waist—and a band of smooth skin that made his mouth suddenly go dry.

As she gathered up her papers, Mark tried to gather up his wits. Some women might be flattered by his appreciative perusal. Abby Warner wasn't one of them. Doing his best to act natural, he propped one shoulder against the door frame.

"I thought I heard someone in here." He hoped she wouldn't notice the slight husky quality in his voice.

She gasped and spun around, one hand flying to the large expanse of exposed skin above the edge of her tank top.

He tried not to stare. "Sorry. I didn't mean to startle you."

"Wh-what are you doing here?"

"I forgot my cell phone."

Abby's gaze dropped for one brief second to his muscular legs before it skittered back to his face, traversing the breadth of his broad chest en route. When she spoke, her smile looked forced and her own voice sounded a bit breathless. "I thought maybe you came in to work."

"It's too hot in here for that. Though the heat hasn't seemed to stop you."

Shrugging, she shuffled the papers in her hand. "I'm used to the heat. I hardly notice it."

Her flushed face, wiped clean of makeup by the humid air, and the damp tendrils of hair that had escaped from her ponytail and now clung to her forehead, invalidated that claim. But he didn't press her. He was enjoying the view too much to introduce an argumentative note to their conversation.

"So why aren't you in Chicago this weekend?"

Her question forced him to refocus. "I have a game this afternoon."

"A game?"

"The pastor from down the street saw me shooting baskets on the church lot and conned me into taking over a boys basketball team until the coach recovers from a broken leg."

"That would be Reverend Andrews." She tipped her head. "You mean you gave up your weekend in Chicago to stay here and coach a kids' basketball game?"

It was no great sacrifice, as far as he was concerned. But he didn't share that with her. "There will be other weekends. Look, I've gotta run. Stay cool."

Without giving her a chance to respond, he turned and headed toward the exit. As he pushed through the door to the lobby, he glanced back. Abby had followed him into the hall, but instead of turning toward her office, she was watching him, her expression confused. When she realized he'd caught her staring, the becoming flush on her cheeks deepened and she twirled around and moved away with a purposeful, no-nonsense stride.

Giving him an incredible view of her trim waist and great legs.

And making him wish he could spend the afternoon with her instead of a bunch of teenage boys.

* * *

"Good job, guys. We'll talk about the game in detail at practice on Tuesday, but for a first effort you should be very happy with the results."

The glowing faces clustered around him two hours later in the corner of the gym were all the proof Mark needed that he'd made the right decision when he'd agreed to coach the team. Not to mention the thanks of the parents, many of whom had stayed around to watch. He couldn't remember when he'd ever felt so appreciated. Or needed.

"Everyone have a ride home?" he asked.

A chorus of affirmative answers came back, and then the kids started to scatter.

"Evan! Wait up."

The lanky teen, his blond hair spiky with sweat after the game, slowed his retreat at Mark's summons and turned—but he stayed where he was.

With the ball still hooked under his arm, Mark didn't rush to close the distance between them. This was new territory for him, and he wasn't sure about his approach. But something was wrong with this kid. He'd only met him on Tuesday, but the boy had been eager and talented. After the impromptu tutoring session following practice, Mark had been surprised at Evan's skill with the spin maneuver two days later. As a result, he'd expected great things from him today.

Instead of the shining, up-and-coming star he'd expected, however, Evan had been listless and inattentive. He'd missed passes and throws that he'd nailed at the last practice. Maybe it was none of Mark's business, but he couldn't just let him walk away.

"I can't stay. I hitched a ride with Justin, and his dad's ready to leave." Evan edged away as Mark approached.

"I won't hold you up. I just wanted to ask if everything is okay. You seemed a little distracted out there today."

"Sorry."

When the boy didn't offer anything more, Mark tried again. "Listen, if there's a problem, I don't mind listening."

Shoulders slumping, Evan shook his head and averted his eyes. "Thanks anyway. I gotta run."

Without waiting for Mark to respond, the boy bolted.

"Do I detect a problem?"

At the sound of Reverend Andrews's voice, Mark turned. The minister had attended the game as a show of support for the boys, impressing Mark once again with his kindness and genuine caring. Maybe he could offer a clue about Evan's problem. "Something's eating him," Mark said.

"I noticed. He seemed out of it on the court today."

"Any idea what's going on? I'd pegged him as one of my high-potential players, but he sure didn't live up to that today."

"The family is having some problems. Evan's father was laid off from his factory job in Rolla about ten months ago and is still unemployed. To complicate matters, Evan's mom was severely injured in a car accident a couple of years back and has been in and out of the hospital ever since. She was re-hospitalized yesterday with chest pain, which the doctors think is related to the punctured lung she suffered in the accident."

No wonder Evan had been preoccupied. "How is she doing?"

"I believe she came home this morning. It's been hard on the kids, though. Evan is the oldest of five, and I think a lot of responsibility has fallen on him to take care of the younger ones during these crisis situations. Plus, the drain on the family finances has been severe. I'm afraid the situation may be getting desperate. The church helps, but our resources are limited. And it takes far too long to cut through government red tape to get timely assistance." The man shook his head, his expression troubled. "It's impossible to address all the needs out there. I wish we could do more."

It was hard for Mark to imagine the situation the pastor had described. By the time he was old enough to remember, his family had been well-off. The very notion of money problems was foreign to him. But he was the exception, he realized, thinking of Abby's simple existence and the financial issues at the *Gazette*. Most of the world hadn't lived the privileged life he'd enjoyed.

"Well, putting Evan's problems aside for a moment, I want to thank you again for stepping in," the minister said. "It's been a great blessing. The boys and their families are grateful, and they made a fine showing for their first attempt."

"Thanks." Mark found it a bit harder to switch gears. "But we have lots of work ahead."

"I have every confidence in you." The pastor extended his hand and Mark returned his firm clasp. "Now go enjoy the rest of your day."

Good advice. But for some reason, Mark suspected it wouldn't be easy to follow.

The steady, rhythmic beat of sneakers against concrete as Abby jogged down the country road was soothing, and for the first time since her encounter with Mark that morning the tension in her shoulders began to ease.

Though she'd tried to refocus on her work after his unexpected visit, it had been an exercise in futility. After a couple of frustrating hours, she'd closed up shop for the day. And tried to deal with the questions his visit had raised.

Like, how in the world had Reverend Andrews convinced Mark to coach the basketball team? And to give up his cherished weekends in Chicago? Weekends that surely included visits with his many female acquaintances—who called often, according to Molly.

The Mark who had first come to the *Gazette* wouldn't have done that. At least she didn't think so. Yet in recent weeks she'd been forced to acknowledge that her original assessment of him as a slacker and playboy might have been a bit hasty—and harsh. She couldn't fault his work ethic. He put in a full eight hours, and according to Joe he often took work back to the B and B, arriving the next morning with a list of questions he'd compiled the night before. And despite his initial resistance, he'd been a good sport about the shadowing assignment—even attending late-night press approvals when asked.

Still, none of that explained why he was willing to take on the basketball job. Or give up his weekends.

Even more disconcerting, however, was her growing awareness of him as more than a business associate.

Until this morning, she'd done a good job ignoring her attraction to him. But when he'd appeared in the copy room, all muscles and masculinity, she hadn't been able to pretend any longer. The man appealed to her. And though her experience with men was limited, she hadn't mistaken the look in his eyes. He'd been attracted to her, too.

Of course, it could simply be that he was stuck in the boonies and eligible females were in short supply. As the only available woman in the newsroom, it was natural that he would gravitate toward her. It didn't mean anything except that he was bored and wanted a little female companionship.

As for herself, she'd focused all of her energy and attention on the *Gazette* for ten years. There had been no time for romance—nor many potential partners, if there had been. But that didn't mean she was immune to male charms. It was only normal that when a handsome, eligible man came along, she'd respond.

And Mark Campbell was both handsome and eligible.

Still, if the attraction was purely physical, she could have resisted.

But Mark had substance. He worked hard. He'd generously offered to coach the basketball team, whatever his motivation. He treated the *Gazette* staff members with respect. And he seemed to care about her.

How was she supposed to resist that?

Yet she had to. Her parents' marriage was all the proof she needed that a successful relationship between her and Mark was highly improbable. Their backgrounds were too different, just as her parents' had been.

As she drew in a deep, cleansing breath of the fresh country air, Abby wished she could have known her parents during their whirlwind college romance, when their love was fresh and new. But as far back as she could remember, their marriage had been troubled.

It wasn't hard to figure out why. Her mother had been the pampered daughter of a prominent banker in San Francisco, who'd grown up with the best of everything, including haute couture clothes and trips abroad. She'd hated Oak Hill's small-town mentality, decried the lack of cultural opportunities, complained about the dearth of social events. And she'd resented her husband's immersion in the *Gazette.* As the years passed, she went home—as she'd always referred to San Francisco—more and more often for visits.

That had hurt her father, Abby knew. She'd seen the sadness—and resignation—in his eyes. Too late, he'd realized that he could never give his wife the kind of life she wanted. Content with a simple existence, he had assumed she understood that he could offer her no more than that. She, on the other hand, had pictured the *San Francisco Chronicle,* but had gotten the *Oak Hill Gazette.* She felt misled; he'd felt as if he'd failed her.

Opposites attracting and love conquering all might sound good in romance novels, but Abby had seen little evidence of that happening in real life. Which was why she couldn't get carried away with her feelings for Mark.

Besides, he'd be gone in a few weeks, she reminded herself. And after he left, she could—

All at once, the ground beneath her feet seemed to undulate and the world tilted. A wave of dizziness swept over her, and her steady gait faltered. Jolted, she jogged for a few more halting steps, until a debilitating weakness robbed her legs of their strength and she stumbled. As fear tightened her throat, she slowed to a walk, groping for a tree at the edge of the road. Clutching the trunk, she eased herself to the ground and peered at her watch.

The numbers faded in and out of focus, but it took only a couple of seconds for her suspicions to be confirmed. She'd overdone her exercise. She'd been so intent on trying to sort through her chaotic thoughts that she'd lost track of the time.

And she'd committed another no-no, as well, she realized with a sick feeling in the pit of her stomach. She'd wandered far afield from her regular in-town route, tempted by the shady, secluded side road that had beckoned with the promise of uninterrupted, contemplative quiet.

Now she was paying the price.

Fumbling in her pocket, she willed her uncooperative fingers to grasp the life-saving cellophane, but they refused. Her panic escalating, she raised her head to search the deserted road, hoping to spot a car. But there was no one in sight.

It was up to her, she realized. And she didn't have a whole lot of time.

Closing her eyes, she sent a silent plea heavenward. *Please, Lord, help me!*

Instead of taking the most direct route back to Oak Hill from the adjacent town, Mark had opted to meander on some side roads, hoping the peace and quiet of the early autumn day would seep into his soul.

It hadn't.

As he drove through the rolling countryside, he couldn't get the conversation with Reverend Andrews out of his head. If anything, he was more unsettled than ever. Not only by the problems in Evan's family but by a sudden strong desire to help. It was unlike anything he'd ever experienced.

Confused, Mark lifted one hand from the wheel and raked his fingers through his hair. Over the years, he'd been solicited by countless charities and always responded with a generous contribution. But he'd never dwelt on the problems of the people his donations would assist. Why was this case different?

The answer came to him in a flash of insight: he had a face to go with the need. In the past, he'd never felt a personal connection to those in distress. Writing a check had been a simple way to dispense with any obligations he might feel to return some of the bounty with which he'd been blessed.

Yet all at once it didn't seem like enough. There must be thousands of families out there like Evan's that needed immediate assistance to get through temporary crises. As Reverend Andrews had pointed out, the church was doing what it could, but resources were too limited to address all the needs.

The germ of an idea began to percolate in Mark's mind as he swung onto a country lane bordered by towering oak trees. Turning off the air-conditioning and lowering his window, he drew a deep, calming breath of the warm, fresh air. The gentle pace of country life was growing on him. Not that he'd want to live here permanently—he enjoyed the museums and fine restaurants and theater in the city too much for that. But as a relaxing getaway, this was hard to beat.

The restful scene was just beginning to soothe his soul when he caught a glimpse through the trees of a solitary jogger up ahead, around the next bend. A woman, darting in and out of his view through the foliage along the side of the road. He realized it was Abby, recognizing her shorts and tank top from that morning.

He slowed the car so he could watch her a bit longer before she caught sight of him. She had a healthy stride, running with the same precision, determination and focus she gave to her job, her ponytail swinging back and forth in an easy rhythm. An appreciative smile curved his lips as he focused on those attractive legs .

At first it didn't alarm him when she slowed her pace. But as her movements changed from fluid and graceful to jerky and erratic, a warning bell sounded in his mind and his smile flattened. When she suddenly lurched toward a tree at the side of the road, his heart skipped a beat. Some foliage obscured his view as his car moved down the road, and when next he caught sight of her, she was sitting on the ground, propped against the tree trunk, her head bowed.

A surge of adrenaline shot through him as he gunned the motor and raced toward her. When he drew close, he jammed on the brakes and jumped out of the car almost before it had come to a complete stop, then took off at a sprint.

Dropping down on one knee beside her, he gripped her shoulders. "Abby? What's wrong?"

When she didn't raise her head, he gave her a gentle shake and attempted to rein in his escalating panic. "Abby!"

At last his presence seemed to register. She lifted her head to stare at him, her eyes vacant and unfocused in a too-pale face. He could feel her trembling beneath his fingers. Though her skin felt cool and clammy, there was a thin film of sweat on her forehead.

Something was terribly wrong.

"Help me." As she whispered the words, Abby lifted her hand and held it out to him. A cellophane-wrapped hard candy lay in her unsteady palm.

Confusion and panic merged in Mark's mind. In the midst of some kind of medical emergency, she wanted to eat candy? It was clear that whatever illness had gripped her body had muddled her mind, as well. Realizing that she needed more help than he could provide, he reached for the cell phone clipped to his shorts. His fingers were poised to punch in 911 when she tugged on his arm, her expression frantic, and pointed to her foot.

A thin silver chain circled her slender ankle, and he

leaned close to examine it. The word *diabetic* jumped out at him.

All at once the pieces fell into place. Abby had diabetes. She was having some kind of diabetic reaction. And he didn't have a clue how to help her.

Fear clutched at his gut as she thrust the candy at him again.

"Open."

At her faint but urgent instruction, he grabbed the piece of hard candy and, with fumbling fingers, managed to rip off the cellophane. When he eased it between her lips, she began to chew vigorously. "More," she managed to say after a few seconds, indicating the pocket of her shorts.

Mark dug out five more pieces of candy, unwrapping them as fast as his suddenly clumsy fingers would allow. She downed them in rapid succession, then leaned back against the trunk of the tree and closed her eyes. Mark took her hand, unsure now whether the trembling was hers or his. He felt as unsteady as she looked.

"Should I call 911?" he asked, cocooning her cold fingers between his.

"No. G-give me a minute."

To his surprise, it didn't take a whole lot more than that for her breathing to even out and some of her color to return. When she opened her eyes a few minutes later, they were clear, focused—and grateful.

"Talk about coming along at the perfect moment." Her voice, though still soft, was much stronger. "I don't even want to think about what might have happened if you hadn't."

Neither did he. "Are you sure you're going to be okay?"

"Yes. The candy did the trick. At least enough to get me home."

"I'll drive you."

"Thanks." She gave him a grateful smile. "I could probably make it on my own, but I'd rather not try."

"I'm heading back to town, anyway. Do you feel up to walking over to my car?"

"Sure. I think so."

He didn't miss the caveat. Rising, he grasped her hands, pulling her up in one smooth, effortless motion. When she swayed, his arms went around her waist and she clutched his shirt.

"Sorry." She tried to laugh, but couldn't quite pull it off. "My legs feel a little rubbery."

"We'll take it slow and easy."

As they moved toward his car, Abby leaned on him heavily and maintained a fierce grip on his arm. It seemed to require every bit of her concentration to put one foot in front of the other, and tremors still rippled through her body. He tightened his hold, giving her a comforting, reassuring squeeze. "We're almost there."

When they reached the passenger side, he eased her down and secured her seat belt before closing the door. After sliding into the driver's seat, he looked over to find that she'd let her head drop back against the headrest. Her eyes were closed, but since the steady rise and fall of her chest told him that her breathing was regular, he didn't disturb her.

The drive back to town was a silent one—and that was fine with Mark. If his thoughts had been tangled earlier because of Evan's situation, they were now chaotic, thanks to the woman beside him. He needed a few minutes to regroup.

Since this morning, he'd been confused by his reaction to her at the copy machine. He'd tried to attribute it simply to a normal reaction to an attractive woman. Yet he knew it went way beyond that. Abby was so much more than a pretty face. She was smart and strong and passionate about the things she believed in. She worked hard, cared about her employees and sacrificed to keep her family's dream alive. She had a strong faith that had sustained her. Unlike many of the women he'd dated, who went out of their way to appear helpless, Abby was a capable woman who didn't need the man in her life to hold her up.

But today he'd seen a whole new side of her. A vulnerable side. One that brought out unfamiliar—but not unwelcome—feelings of protectiveness in him. For someone who'd avoided commitment like the plague, it was disconcerting to discover that he didn't mind the idea of Abby depending on him.

But on the heels of that discovery came fear.

It was the same fear he'd felt when he'd learned that Bobby Mitchell had leukemia. When he'd waited in the emergency room with his father and brother after his mother suffered her fatal cerebral hemorrhage.

The kind of cold, gripping fear that twists your gut as you stand by, helpless, while forces over which you have no control steal the life from someone you love.

Mark had been there not just once but twice. And he didn't want to go there again. It was why he'd avoided commitments. Why he'd distanced himself from him family. If you didn't care, you couldn't get hurt.

It was also the reason he had to distance himself from Abby. It would be far too easy to care about this woman. He couldn't let that happen—especially in light of her illness.

But even as he vowed not to let her touch his heart, he knew it was too late.

Because she already had.

Chapter Nine

Mark didn't disturb Abby until they reached the outskirts of town. Then he had no choice.

"Abby?" He spoke in a muted tone to avoid startling her. "I need some directions."

Her eyelids flickered open, and when she turned to him he was relieved to see that most of her color had returned. She sat up and took a second to orient herself. "Make a left at the next corner. You'll come to Healy in about half a mile. Turn right. My house is the last one, at the end of the street."

Within a couple of minutes, Mark pulled to a stop in front of a modest white-frame bungalow that was dwarfed by the huge, stately oak trees lining the street and dotting the expansive lawn. A porch swing hung from the rafters of a small veranda, reached via three concrete steps. A large fern in a hanging pot added a graceful touch to the shady refuge, and the steps were flanked by colorful urns filled with petunias and ornamental grasses. The nearest neighbors were a couple of empty lots away on the dead-end street, giving the house a very private setting.

As he set the brake, Mark surveyed the charming—but tiny—house where Abby had grown up. Recalling his family's spacious suburban ranch home, Mark couldn't imagine living in such close quarters.

When Abby started to open her door, Mark restrained her, his touch gentle but firm. "Let me."

Before she could protest, he was out the door and circling the car. When he reached for her, Abby swung her legs to the ground and gripped his warm, solid hand. Once on her feet, she checked her balance, then smiled.

"Much better. In fact, almost as good as new," she pronounced.

She did look more like herself, Mark acknowledged as he scrutinized her. Her color was good, her deep green eyes were clear, her trembling had subsided. Some of the tension in his shoulders eased.

"Does that kind of thing happen very often?" Mark asked.

"Only once before, not long after I was diagnosed several months ago, when my endocrinologist was still trying to regulate my medication. I brought today's problem on myself."

"How so?"

Tilting her head, Abby regarded him. "How much do you know about diabetes?"

"Almost nothing."

"I have what's known as type 2. That means my pancreas produces some insulin—which the body needs in order to use glucose—but it either doesn't produce enough or my body isn't able to recognize the insulin and use it properly. So I have to regulate the balance between insulin and glucose levels through diet, exercise and medication. Today the balance got out of whack and my blood-sugar levels dropped. The technical term is hypoglycemia."

"But why did it happen?"

"Too much exercise and not enough food. I should have eaten more to counterbalance the energy I was using."

"The candy seemed to help."

"It got me through the crisis. But I need to get inside and check my blood-sugar levels. And I'll probably have to eat something else."

"Is there someone you want to call to come and stay with you a while? Dale, maybe?"

The question seemed to surprise her as much as it did him. But at least her blank look silenced the speculations that had plagued him since the day the suspicious package arrived at the *Gazette*. "Why would I call Dale?"

"You two seem…close."

An inquisitive expression flitted through her eyes, perceptive enough to warm the back of his neck. "Dale and I grew up together. He was a friend of my brother's, and I always thought of him as sort of a second older brother. But he has his own issues to deal with, including the challenges of raising a four-year-old alone. I don't need to add to his problems. Besides, I'm fine now."

Mark didn't want to know about the sheriff's problems. He had too much on his plate as it was. And as for her condition, he wasn't convinced she was fine. Even though she seemed okay now, less then twenty minutes ago he'd been ready to call 911.

"Look, maybe you ought to check in with your doctor."

"I might give him a ring Monday."

"What if this happens again before then?"

"It won't. As long as I'm careful." She angled her wrist and checked her watch.

He got the message. Stepping aside, he jammed his palms into the back pockets of his shorts, stretching the fabric of his T-shirt taut against his broad chest. For an instant, Abby's gaze dropped there. Then she looked away.

"T-thanks again," she murmured, not quite meeting his eyes.

"I'm glad I happened to be in the neighborhood. See you Monday."

As Mark slid into the driver's seat, Abby backed up. She watched as he maneuvered the car on the dead-end street, waved as he headed toward town, then walked toward her house.

But when Mark flicked a glance in his rearview mirror, he discovered she was still watching him from the shadows of her porch, much as she had done this morning at the *Gazette* office.

On one level, that pleased him. On another, it scared him. He was treading on dangerous ground with Abby.

And he knew that if he wanted to protect his heart, he had to muster the resolve to keep his distance.

* * *

Abby pricked her finger with the lancet, squeezed a drop of blood onto the test strip and put the strip into the glucometer. She peered at the reading. Still a bit low but nothing a snack wouldn't fix.

As for her heart…that was harder to fix, she reflected, as she ripped open a pack of peanut butter crackers. She supposed she could try avoiding Mark, but at this point she wasn't sure that would work. He was nowhere in sight now, yet the mere memory of his warm touch, his concerned eyes, his genuine caring, was enough to wreak havoc on her heart.

And the fact that he'd seemed a bit jealous of Dale hadn't helped.

She could be wrong about the jealousy, though. His query about the sheriff could have been prompted by simple human kindness, nothing more. After all, she'd been in pretty bad shape when he'd found her. For someone unfamiliar with hypoglycemia, the episode would have been frightening in its swiftness and intensity. And for the uninitiated, the equally rapid recovery would be hard to grasp. He might have been afraid to leave her alone for fear of a relapse.

Yet she sensed that Mark's interest went beyond that of a simple Good Samaritan. She suspected it bordered on romantic.

Just as hers did.

But that wasn't good. The look on Mark's face when he'd found her in the throes of a hypoglycemia attack had reminded her of her father's constant worry, as well as his grief after her mother died far too young from the disease. Illness put a strain on relationships. As did differences in backgrounds. Add in the fact that Mark and his family were trying to take away her family legacy, and you had a recipe for disaster.

In her head, Abby knew that. Her heart, however, wasn't convinced. The simple truth was that as her professional opinion of the Campbell Publishing heir had shifted, so had her personal feelings. Where once he'd represented a danger to the *Gazette,* he now embodied an even more potent threat. One she felt even less equipped to deflect.

Because not only was his presence putting her family legacy in peril, it was jeopardizing her heart, as well.

"Okay, guys, that'll do it for tonight."

Mark tucked the basketball under his arm and surveyed the boys. Even though they'd moved practice to five o'clock instead of six, dusk was already falling. But the fading light hadn't dimmed the boys' spirits. The team members had been pumped since their first game ten days ago, and the improvement after a mere half dozen or so practices was remarkable. Every team member had made great strides.

Except Evan.

As the angled evening light threw the boys' faces into relief, most looked eager and excited and carefree. But the shadows highlighted the creases on Evan's brow and his discouraged demeanor—both reinforced by the dejected slump of his shoulders. The boy looked far too old for his years, and a pang of sympathy tightened Mark's heart.

"Don't forget—we're moving the practices to the school gym starting Thursday. I'll see you all then," Mark dismissed them.

A chorus of "See yas" and "Thanks" echoed as the boys dispersed, many to waiting cars, others on foot. Evan was in the latter group, and Mark watched him depart, his expression troubled.

"Good practice."

At Reverend Andrews's voice, Mark turned. "I didn't know you were watching."

"I just caught the end. You've worked wonders with them in a very short time."

"All except Evan."

"That's a tough case." The pastor looked after the boy, who had been joined by one of the other team members as he trudged away. "I spoke with his father after Sunday services. He's a good man, and he's doing his best, but I think he's at his wit's end. They're barely scraping by."

Mark hadn't had a chance to give much thought to the idea that had started to niggle at his brain after the practice game, but as the minister continued, it resurfaced.

"Anyway, I offered to raid the church coffers again, but he said they'd be okay for a couple of weeks. Then he told me in confidence that Evan had given him his space fund to help with household expenses." The man shook his head. "Evan is one special kid."

"Space fund?" Mark stared at the minister.

The man smiled. "Sorry. You wouldn't know about that. But it's kind of legendary in Oak Hill. Evan has always had an avid interest in astronomy, and he's been saving his earnings from grass cutting, leaf raking and odd jobs for two years so he could go to space camp in Huntsville next March, over spring break. It's an educational program at the U.S. Space & Rocket Center in Alabama."

"Yeah, I've heard of it." Mark's throat tightened with emotion and he averted his head, staring at the long shadow cast by the church as the orange sun disappeared behind it.

How odd that Evan, just like Bobby Mitchell, had funneled every spare penny into a space fund. But Bobby's dream of going to space camp hadn't been shattered by family financial hardship, like Evan's. Instead, leukemia had robbed him of that chance. A senseless illness that had cut short a life filled with potential. An illness Mark had never been able to accept as God's will, as had been suggested to him at the time. How could the loving, caring God his parents worshipped end a young life so abruptly and inflict such raw grief and irreconcilable loss on those left behind? It hadn't made sense then, and it didn't make sense twenty-plus years later.

"Mark?"

Mark pulled himself back to the present. The minister seemed to be waiting for him to speak, but Mark didn't know what to say.

When he remained silent, the man took the lead. "You look troubled."

"I'm worried about Evan. And his family."

Tilting his head, Reverend Andrews studied him. "Why do I sense that it's more than that?"

The question didn't require a detailed answer. Mark could brush it off if he chose. And he didn't think the pastor would push the issue. Yet the man had opened the door for further discussion, if Mark wanted to walk through.

Once before, he'd been tempted to share his feelings with Reverend Andrews. There was an innate goodness about him, a kindness, that invited confidences. That suggested he could listen with understanding and empathy, withholding judgment.

Mark had resisted the temptation last time. But much had changed since then. He was having more and more difficulty dealing with a slew of unexpected emotions. Not the least of which were his conflicting feelings—and growing attraction—for Abby.

Though he didn't intend to discuss that dilemma tonight, perhaps he could talk with this man about the most painful period in his past. Persistent reminders of it were beginning to convince him that the long-buried interlude might have played a far bigger role in shaping his life that he'd ever realized.

"I know a nice quiet place to talk." The minister withdrew a set of keys from his pocket and jingled them as he inclined his head toward the church.

Torn, Mark looked again toward the white clapboard structure with the soaring steeple. As the shadow of the church crept across the parking lot toward them, Mark thought of Abby's quiet faith. She'd alluded to her trust in the Lord once, and it seemed to sustain her through her trials. He thought of his father, who'd built a publishing empire based on the principles of his faith. Of his brother, who'd chosen a faith-based career that offered far less in monetary rewards than many other options. Of Evan Lange and his family, who continued to worship despite the difficulties that had beset them.

Had he been missing some essential truth about faith that might help him deal with the difficulties in his life? If so, could this man help him discover it?

Raking his fingers through his hair, Mark looked back at the minister. "I haven't been in a church for quite a while. Like I told you at our first meeting, pastor, I'm not very religious. Though I'm beginning to wish I was."

"Regular church attendance isn't a requirement for entering the house of God," the man told him with a smile. "Nor is it necessarily an indication of spirituality. I hate to say it, but there are members of every congregation who never miss a Sunday service, who give all the outward appearances of being good Christians, but who fail to live the tenets of their faith the rest of the week. The problem with them is that they think they're doing everything they're supposed to do by showing up on the Lord's day. I'd rather have a few more like you, who recognize and acknowledge the lack of faith in their lives, but feel a call to deepen their relationship with the Lord.

"That said, however, this isn't a conversion session, Mark. I'm willing to listen merely as a friend if you think talking about whatever is bothering you might help. The church happens to be convenient—and quiet. We could accomplish the same thing in the city park if it was closer."

With sudden decision, Mark nodded. "Okay. I'll meet you inside."

While Mark deposited the basketball and other equipment in his car, Reverend Andrews unlocked the church. When Mark rejoined him, the man was seated in a pew near the back. Mark slid onto the polished oak bench beside him and looked around.

It was a small, simple church, classic in design, with tall, clear windows that ran the length of each side. Electric brass candelabras hung over a center aisle that ended at the raised sanctuary. Dimmed, their muted light combined with the glow of the setting sun to give the space a mellow, peaceful feeling.

"Nice," Mark commented.

"I agree. It's a worthy place to worship, thanks to the support of the congregation. The members are very good about pitching in to maintain both the physical and spiritual structure of the church. They always step in when the need arises. Like the situation with Evan's family. One of the women organized a casserole program, and the ladies have been providing meals at least four nights a week for the family. Even busy women like Abby Warner, who already have their hands full with plenty of other challenge and demands, are participating. I'm always touched by such outpourings of generosity."

"Abby cooks for the Langes?"

"She takes her turn, like all the rest. She's an amazing woman."

"Yes, she is."

The minister's eyes narrowed a bit, and Mark felt hot

color steal up his neck as he met the man's insightful gaze. He wasn't ready to talk about Abby. So he was relieved when the man draped an arm over the back of the pew and changed the subject.

"I didn't mean to be pushy out there on the parking lot, but I couldn't help noticing that you seem very disturbed about Evan's situation. Perhaps more than might be normal given that you don't know him well yet and have never met his family."

Clasping his hands between his knees, Mark leaned forward and stared down at his clenched knuckles. "I am upset. It's been on my mind since the first game, when you explained the problem. But our conversation a few minutes ago…it triggered memories of a very difficult time from my past."

"The recent past?"

"No. This happened twenty-one years ago. When I was thirteen. About Evan's age." He shook his head. "I thought I'd put it to rest and moved on. But it all came rushing back out in the parking lot. The odd thing is, over the past few weeks that's happened several times. What surprises me is how painful the memories are even after all this time."

"Traumatic events can have that effect on people. And if they occur when we're young, the impact can be even more dramatic, leaving us with lots of unresolved questions and issues. What dredged them up just now?"

"The space camp reference." Taking a deep breath, Mark lifted his head and stared toward the large cross that dominated the sanctuary. "My best friend as a kid developed an avid interest in astronomy when we were about ten and decided he wanted to be an astronaut. Bobby was in awe of the universe, and he made the stars and the planets sound so exciting that he swept me along on his dream. He started dragging me out to the backyard in the middle of the night to look through his telescope, and pretty soon I wanted to be an astronaut, too. I'm not sure I would have followed through, but I have no doubt he would have—if he'd had the chance."

"Why didn't he?"

A muscle clenched in Mark's jaw. "He died when we were thirteen. Leukemia."

There was silence for a moment before Reverend Andrews responded. "I'm more sorry than I can say. For both of you."

The minister's sincere, compassionate tone tightened Mark's throat. "Yeah. Me, too. We were inseparable. From the time we could walk and talk we were best buddies. We never even had a fight. Not one. When he got leukemia, it never occurred to me that he wouldn't survive. With all his spunk and spirit, I was convinced he'd beat the disease. He felt the same way.

"Anyway, we both started praying—that was back in the days when I still believed that God was in His heaven and all was right with the world. A lot of other people were praying, too. I figured God had to listen to all those voices. That surely He wouldn't let a kid like Bobby die. Even when things started to get really bad I kept believing. I just knew God would save him, even if it took a miracle."

The expression on Mark's face hardened, and bitterness etched his voice, like acid on metal. "I was wrong.

Bobby died. But I wouldn't accept it. I wouldn't even go the funeral. For months afterward, I was distraught. I realize now I could have used some help, but in those days no one thought much about grief counseling for kids. You just got over it, you know? Except I didn't. The sense of loss was overwhelming. So was the anger. How could God let that happen? I kept asking that question, but no one had any answers that made sense to me. In the end, I stopped going to church and turned my back on the Lord."

Drawing a ragged breath, he propped his elbows on his knees and pressed his fingertips to his temples. "Maybe in time I might have gotten over that. But eight months later my mother died of a cerebral hemorrhage."

"I'm sure that multiplied your sense of loss exponentially."

"Yeah, it did. My whole world seemed to be caving in, but there was no one I could turn to for comfort or consolation. My brother was too little to grasp the extent of my trauma, and my dad was too mired in his own grief to help me deal with mine. I felt like I was drowning. The only way I could stay afloat was to bury that whole period of my life so deep it could never rise to the surface. And that worked for many years. To the point that I thought it had lost the power to hurt me.

"But I was wrong about that, too. It's still there. And I'm beginning to think it's had a far greater impact on my life than I ever imagined." His voice caught on the last word, and he sucked in a ragged breath.

Even before the minister spoke, Mark felt deep

caring and compassion and a sense of connection in the hand that was placed on his shoulder.

"I'm sorry for your losses, Mark."

Blinking back the sudden moisture in his eyes, Mark turned to the man. "So why does God let good people die so young?"

The question was torn right from his heart, and the minister returned his anguished look with one that was steady, direct and honest. "There's no answer to that question, Mark. People have struggled with it through the ages, and many have turned away from their faith because of it, as you did.

"But I can tell you this. While God blessed us with intellect, our intelligence isn't great enough to allow us to grasp the mysteries of His ways. Trying to understand the mind of God is like attempting to audit the books of the most complicated business in the world with nothing more than a pencil and paper. Or trying to build a spaceship with only a hammer and nails. We aren't equipped for the job. It's an exercise in futility."

The man leaned forward, his expression earnest. "Once we learn to accept that and to recognize the most essential truth—that God loves us and sent His Son to save us—the quest for answers becomes far less of an obsession. We can learn to trust in God's goodness without fully understanding His ways. And that trust opens our hearts to the many gifts with which we are blessed and allows us to face the future with hope."

As Mark pondered the minister's words, he turned to stare at the cross. He'd never thought of the events of his life in quite that context. He'd tried to make sense of them instead of accepting them as part of the mystery of God's plan. As a numbers man, he was used to definitive answers, accustomed to things adding up. Two plus two always equaled four. Yet life wasn't that precise. Or that predictable. It had been a losing battle to try and make it conform to an exacting mathematical model.

But he'd lost in other ways, as well, he acknowledged. When his mother was taken, the place deep inside him where hope and ambition and faith were barely clinging to life had died, too. And he'd shut down. Going forward, he'd operated on a simple philosophy: don't kill yourself working for something that could be snatched away tomorrow. Don't form attachments that could be severed in an instant. Don't honor an uncaring God.

For twenty-one years he'd lived his life by those rules. But he hadn't been happy, he acknowledged. Though he'd gone through the motions of his glamorous lifestyle, an emptiness had plagued his days. As had a soul-deep loneliness that echoed in his heart. If asked what his life stood for, he'd be hard-pressed to find an answer. He could list no notable achievements. And he could count on one hand the people who loved him. Not much to show for thirty-four years of living.

But if the minister was right, there was still hope. He could put his trust in the Lord and embrace tomorrow, accept the gifts that God sent his way—including love—and do his part to brighten a few lives. In other words, live with purpose rather than just exist.

It was a new concept for him, one predicated on establishing a relationship with the Lord. And that wouldn't be easy. Not after years of estrangement. Yet despite the difficulties inherent in that journey, a tiny ember of optimism began to smolder deep in his soul. Recalling the old saying "A journey of a thousand miles begins with the first step," Mark knew that he had taken that first step today, thanks to the man beside him.

Mark looked at Reverend Andrews and extended his hand. "Thank you."

The man took it in a firm clasp. "Anytime. Talking things through can often work miracles."

Mark had to agree.

Chapter Ten

Abby was avoiding him.

As Mark headed toward the coffeemaker in the *Gazette's* break room, he noted that her office door was once again closed—as it had been since the hypoglycemia incident the weekend before. Add in the fact that she'd also sent him on a number of shadowing assignments away from the office, and the message was clear. She didn't want to see him.

A few weeks ago, Mark would have been glad that she was distancing herself. But since his talk with Reverend Andrews he was rethinking a lot of things in his life. Including the reasons he'd avoided relationships all these years. Abbey's diabetes had thrown him, but after hours on the Internet researching the disease, he'd concluded that while it could be unpleasant, it was manageable. He was pretty sure he could live with the risks, despite the medical traumas in his past.

However, Abby wasn't giving him a chance to find out. Since their encounter on Saturday, she'd made herself as scarce as a Starbucks in Oak Hill. The question was, why?

It didn't take a genius to come up with a couple of reasons. For one, he was the enemy. Given a favorable report by him, Campbell Publishing was poised to take over the helm of the *Gazette* and end the Warner legacy.

But Abby was a smart woman. She had to know that if Campbell Publishing didn't acquire the paper, it would fall prey to another conglomerate—or go under. And the *Gazette* could face a far worse fate than being drawn into the fold of the principled operation his father had created. He had a feeling she knew that.

Still, the loss of her family heritage, which she regarded as a sacred trust, would be deeply distressing. And his role in the takeover wouldn't endear him to her.

Then there was the fact that they'd gotten off on the wrong foot. He was well aware that she'd written him off as a lightweight when they'd met. But in the weeks he'd been in Oak Hill, he'd worked hard. He'd taken on all the shadowing assignments without complaint, despite the disruption in his auditing schedule. He'd even gotten involved in the community by agreeing to coach the boys' basketball team.

And along the way he'd changed in some profound way that he himself was just beginning to understand. Somehow, he sensed that she'd picked up on that, as well. On more than one occasion he'd seen a glint of admiration in her eyes.

So why was she avoiding him? Unless…was it possible she wasn't attracted to him?

Stunned by the possibility, Mark's hand stilled on the

coffeepot. None of the women he'd ever pursued had been immune to his dark good looks. Not that he was vain about his appearance. After all, he couldn't claim any credit for the way he looked. It was merely the hand he'd been dealt. But the fact was, he'd always turned women's heads.

With the possible exception of Abby's.

Pouring his coffee, he grabbed the hot-off-the-press Wednesday edition of the *Gazette* and headed back to the conference room, noting that her door was still closed. As he mulled over his dilemma, he gave the paper a distracted scan—until the headline for the final installment of Abby's hate-crimes series popped off the page and snagged his attention.

Here we go again, he thought, his gut clenching as he read the article.

Like the original editorial and part one of the series, the piece was objective, well-researched, thoughtful and articulate. Yet he was sure it would again incite the person who had taken issue with the previous pieces.

Mark admired Abby for her courageous coverage. It was no wonder the *Gazette* had won numerous awards through the years, in addition to the Pulitzer prize. And there was no question that Abby was following in the footsteps of her predecessors, carrying on their tradition of sharp, insightful journalism.

His father would be impressed, Mark knew. It was because of articles like this that the *Gazette* had come to Spencer Campbell's attention. The Campbell Publishing CEO would probably commend her on the series, dashing off one of his trademark "attagirl" e-mails.

Mark supposed he should do the same. And maybe he would.

Just as soon as he figured out how to wash away the taste of fear that even the strong coffee couldn't seem to vanquish.

When Molly passed the conference room door the next Tuesday, Mark's attention zeroed in on the nine-by-twelve manila envelope clutched in her hands. Without stopping to think, he rose and followed her. Though he'd only caught a glimpse or two of Abby since he'd read the hate-crimes piece the previous week, he'd been operating with a sense of heightened awareness. And Molly's posture and expression spelled trouble.

He reached her as she knocked on the closed door of Abby's office, and she turned to him with a worried glance.

"What's up?" He kept his voice low.

"This just arrived. It reminded me—"

"Come in." Abby's muffled voice came from behind the door, and Mark gestured for Molly to enter. He wasn't far behind.

Trepidation flickered across Abby's face as her visitors stepped inside and Mark shut the door behind them. Removing her glasses, she kept her attention on Molly.

"What's going on?"

"This came in the morning mail." Molly held out the envelope. "I haven't opened it, but the printing looks a lot like that first letter you got about the hate-crimes editorial."

Taking the envelope, Abby examined the crude block letters. "There is a similarity." She picked up a letter opener and slit the flap. Her movements were cautious, and Mark thought he detected a slight tremor in her fingers.

With the envelope at arm's length, Abby bowed it to peer inside, then turned it upside down. A copy of the hate-crimes article, perforated with holes, slid across her desk.

Confused, Mark stared at the mutilated newsprint. "I don't get it. What's that supposed to mean?"

"I've seen a pattern like that before." Her face tight with tension, Molly leaned forward for a closer look. "It looks like the targets that Stan sometimes brings home after he practices with his shotgun."

Cold fear gripped Mark's heart. "Call Dale." When Abby opened her mouth, he spoke before she could utter a sound, his expression grim—and unrelenting. "If you don't, I will."

"I'll take care of this, Molly." Pressing her lips together, Abby reached for the phone. "You can go back to work. I'll let you know if Dale thinks there's any reason to worry."

When Molly departed, Mark took a seat in Abby's office. The set of his jaw convinced her he wasn't going to budge until Dale showed up, so she placed the call, then went back to work. Or at least she tried to.

Fifteen minutes later, Dale confirmed Molly's assessment. "The scattered pattern gives it away. As well as the nature of the holes and the variation in size."

"What now?" Mark asked.

Fisting his hands on his hips, Dale sent Abby a concerned look. "I don't like this, Abby. Up until now I was pretty sure we were talking about a prankster. Even the fire at Ali's restaurant was set at night, meaning there was no deliberate intent to hurt someone. But the perpetrator's persistence bothers me. As does the fact that he's got a lethal weapon. Do you have any more coverage planned?"

"No. The final piece ran last Wednesday."

"Good. I'll beef up patrols for the next few days around your house and the *Gazette.*"

"Is that it? Abby could be in serious danger."

At Mark's comment, Dale turned, his probing gaze more insightful than Mark would have liked. "I'm continuing my investigation. And I do have some pretty good leads that I'm following up on." He looked back at Abby. "There was a similar incident with a Middle Eastern business over in Crandall yesterday. It has the earmarks of the same perpetrator. And he left us a few more clues. I think we're closing in. It's just a matter of time."

"Time that Abby might not have," Mark countered.

"We're doing everything we can."

"Can you put a guard on Abby?"

"We don't have the manpower for that."

"I'll be fine," Abby insisted, darting a look at Mark before turning to Dale. "I'll be extra careful and—"

"At least I can follow you home every night for the next few days," Mark cut in.

Startled, she stared at him. "That's not necessary. I'm perfectly capable of—"

"I think it's a good idea, Abby," Dale interrupted.

"Anything we can do to ensure your safety until this is all straightened out is a plus. If Mark's willing to help, I'd suggest you let him."

Outvoted, Abby stared at the two men across from her. She'd done her best to avoid Mark since the jogging incident, and just when she was starting to get her emotions back under control, fate was conspiring to throw the two of them together.

"I stay late," Abby balked, fiddling with some papers on her desk, still refusing to look at him.

Propping a shoulder against the door frame, Mark folded his arms across his chest. "I don't mind waiting."

"What about basketball practice?"

"It's over by six. I'll swing back around when I'm done."

"Give it up, Abby. It's a good plan," Dale said.

Defeated, Abby threw up her hands. "Okay. Fine."

"You're welcome."

At Mark's wry comment, hot color spilled onto Abby's cheeks. It wasn't like her to be ungracious—as Dale's arched brow and speculative look confirmed when she glanced at him.

"Sorry," she amended. "I appreciate the offer. But I do have work to do. So if you gentlemen don't mind…"

"I'll take this along." Dale tucked the tattered paper back into the envelope. "See you two later."

As Dale exited, Abby was left with no choice but to look at Mark. He'd stepped aside to let the sheriff pass and was now regarding her with concern.

"You're still going to be alone in that house every night."

She swallowed past her nervousness. "I have good locks."

His gaze locked on hers. "I'm worried about you, Abby," he said softly.

She wanted to ask why. But she didn't dare. She was too afraid of the answer. His expression was already too eloquent, his tone too warm and personal. Mark cared about her. Too much. More than she could return. She couldn't let this go any further. They'd only end up hurting each other.

"I'll be fine." She tried her best to sound calm and in control, but she couldn't stop the tremor that snaked through her voice.

Instead of responding, Mark looked at her in silence. And from the skeptical tilt of his head, she knew he hadn't bought her reassurance.

Neither had she.

It wasn't that she was worried so much about the physical danger. Caution and common sense would protect her, she was sure.

But when it came to her heart, she didn't seem to have sufficient reserves of those qualities to keep her safe.

By Friday night at seven, as Abby gathered up her purse and the stack of copy she planned to review tomorrow, her nerves were stretched to the breaking point. Though there had been no more incidents related to her hate-crimes coverage, she hadn't been sleeping well. On top of that, Mark had been hovering around since Tuesday, wreaking havoc on her emotions—and her resolve to keep her distance. She needed a long weekend to unwind, decompress and regroup.

As she had come to expect, Mark was still in the conference room when she appeared in the doorway. "This really isn't necessary, you know. I'm sure you have better things to do with your evening than wait around for me."

Looking up, Mark assessed her as she hovered in the doorway, her briefcase clutched to her chest like a shield.

"I didn't mind. I've been working on a special project and I needed access to the Internet."

It was the truth. He'd been using every spare minute to research and flesh out the idea that had been germinating in his mind since he'd learned of the Langes' plight. Though Campbell Publishing's charitable contributions had always been generous, why not create a foundation designed to serve the areas in which the company published papers, with each region overseen by a board of local clergy? That kind of direct, grassroots effort could quickly and effectively identify and provide real assistance to those most in need.

But he also recognized that Campbell Publishing wasn't a charitable entity. He had to make a solid humanitarian *and* business case for his idea—a task that had required exhaustive research. He'd been working on it for weeks, whenever he had a few spare minutes. The hours waiting for Abby had given him the chance to draft a proposal for his father, which he planned to overnight tomorrow.

Her skeptical expression, however, told him she didn't buy his reassurance. "Scout's honor." He grinned and placed his hand over his heart. "Are you ready to leave?"

"Yes."

"Okay. Give me a sec." In one smooth sweep, he slid his papers into his briefcase and shut down his laptop, then rose and followed her to the exit.

A sudden gust of damp, chilly autumn wind sent a pool of rustling leaves whirling around their feet when they stepped outside, and Abby turned up the collar of her lightweight jacket as Mark fell into step beside her. The day had grown much colder as the sun had set, the Indian-summer heat of the afternoon swept away by the fickle end-of-October muse.

Not until she was settled in her car did Mark speak. "I had to park a bit farther away when I came back after lunch. Sit tight a minute."

Without waiting for a response, he strode down the street. Though he wore only a long-sleeved shirt rolled to the elbows, he didn't appear in the least affected by the cold wind, which ruffled his thick, dark hair and whirled around his tall form. When a wave of longing swept over Abby, as powerful as the relentless wind that was stirring up the world on this blustery night, she forced herself to look away.

In ten minutes, she'd be home, she reminded herself. Mark would be gone. She'd have the whole weekend to whip her wayward emotions into shape. And by Monday, she'd be back to normal.

Instead of offering comfort, however, that scenario

depressed her. Because she now equated normal—the life she'd led before Mark—with lonely. And that held no appeal at all.

It happened in the home stretch. And so fast it took several seconds for Mark to react. Not fifty yards from her driveway, Abby swerved abruptly, slid on the damp pavement and plowed into one of the tall oak trees that lined her street.

When the shock passed and his adrenaline kicked in, Mark sped up, then screeched to a stop behind Abby's car. As he raced toward her, his heart pounding, fear choked him. Was this another hypoglycemic episode? That seemed the only possible explanation, since he'd neither seen nor heard anything that could account for her accident. And if she was ill, he knew she needed help. Fast.

Mark yanked open the driver-side door and leaned down. In the car's dim overhead light, he could see that the air bag had inflated, leaving a small, bright red burn mark on Abby's forehead. But other than that, she didn't appear injured. She was staring straight ahead, dazed but conscious, and he touched her cheek.

"Abby?" His voice came out in a hoarse croak, and he cleared his throat. "Are you having another diabetic reaction?"

She drew in a sharp breath, as if her lungs had just kicked back into gear, and turned to him. "No. There was a…a wire stretched across the road. I swerved to avoid it."

Her voice was shaky but coherent, and her eyes were clear and focused. It wasn't a diabetic problem. Relief coursed through him as he slowly let out the breath he hadn't realized he was holding. But they weren't out of the woods yet, he reminded himself. Even though she hadn't been driving fast, she could still be injured.

Reaching out, he took her shoulders in a gentle grip. "Are you hurt? Did you hit your head? Are you dizzy?"

"No. But someone did this, Mark. It was deliberate. There was a wire across the road. I'll show you." She angled her body to exit the car, but Mark pressed her back into the seat.

"Stay put. I'll take a look. Meanwhile, call Dale." He handed her his cell phone.

The fact that she didn't argue told him she was a lot more shaken than she was letting on. Loath to leave her alone, he made quick work of his scouting expedition, then rejoined her.

"Well?" she prompted as he dropped down on the balls of his feet beside her.

"Nothing." He enfolded her cold fingers in his.

She tried not to savor the comfort of his protective clasp. Yet neither did she pull away. "But I saw the wire! I didn't imagine it, Mark."

"I'm sure you didn't. But it's too dark to see much. Maybe Dale can make some sense of it."

And he did. After a quick look at Abby's car and a few queries about her condition, he did some scouting of his own with a high-powered flashlight. Within a couple of minutes he rejoined them, holding a length of magnetic tape.

Clambering out of the car, Abby stared at the metallic strip. "What's that?"

"Tape from an audio cassette. When car headlights

hit it at night, the reflection looks like a wire. I've seen this prank before. Sometimes with far more serious results. If you'd been going much faster, your car would have sustained a lot more damage than a dented bumper and a broken headlight. And so would you."

"I assume this is related to the hate-crimes piece," Mark said.

"That would be a safe bet," Dale concurred. "The timing in relation to the article is too close for coincidence, and no one lives at this end of the street except Abby. It was meant for her."

Suddenly the car shifted, and Abby gasped. Mark's arms went around her in an instinctive protective gesture. He felt her lean into him, the warm softness of her body in sharp contrast to his muscular frame. Dale tensed, and his hand flew to his holster as he peered toward the front of the car. Then his posture relaxed.

"Flat tire," he pointed out.

Leaning forward, Abby stared at the limp rubber in disgust. And took a good look at the damage to the front of her older-model car. With her high-deductible insurance, repairs were going to take a sizable bite out of her meager savings.

"Not much we can do here tonight," Dale said. "Leave the car. You can deal with it tomorrow, in the daylight. Do you want me to call Al and have him stop by to take a look?"

The reliable mechanic had been working on Oak Hill cars for as long as Abby could remember. "Yes. Thanks."

"And you're sure you're not hurt?"

"Yes."

"Okay. I'll take a look around the house before I leave. Hop in." He stepped aside, opening a path to the patrol car.

For a brief instant she didn't move. Nor did Mark retrieve the arm he'd thrown around her shoulders. Seconds ticked by, silent but filled with feelings so intense they were almost tangible. When at last she straightened and eased out from under the weight—and warmth—of his touch, he thought he detected the faintest of sighs, though it was masked by the night breeze.

"Thanks again for following me home," she murmured, a slight breathless quality to her voice.

In the darkness, her face was shadowed and Mark couldn't read her expression. But he sensed that Abby didn't want him to leave. That it had taken every ounce of her willpower to step away from him—because she felt an attraction for him as strong as the one he felt for her.

Testing the waters, he spoke in as casual a tone as he could muster. "I could stay a while, if that would make you feel safer."

"No!" Her reply was swift, almost panicked. "I mean, I'll be fine. Thank you."

Her response was telling. She wanted him to stay. His doubts about whether she was attracted to him were unfounded. But she was afraid. Of what, he wasn't sure. Herself, perhaps. Of giving in to the feelings that had permeated the air mere moments ago. Yet why hold back if she felt the connection as strongly as he did? Why shut him out? Why not explore this thing between them?

Mark had no answers. But as he watched her walk away with Dale, he was determined to find them. Sooner rather than later. Because his time in Oak Hill was fast running out.

Chapter Eleven

I should have gone back to Chicago for the weekend.

That refrain echoed through Mark's mind as he stared out the window of his room at the Oak Hill Inn on Sunday morning, the whole day stretching ahead of him endless and empty. Yesterday's rain hadn't abated, limiting his options for activities. He'd spent Saturday morning reading, then gone into the *Gazette* on the pretense of checking e-mail—but, in truth, he'd hoped to run into Abby. For once, however, the hardworking editor seemed to have given herself the day off.

After surfing the Internet for a couple of hours while he'd waited for FedEx to pick up the proposal for his father, he'd taken in the movie in town. It wasn't any better than his first viewing in Chicago, but at least it passed a couple of hours. He'd tried to get a last-minute reservation at the gourmet restaurant at the Oak Hill Inn, but it had been booked solid. Dinner at Gus's had been the highlight of his day.

Pretty pathetic.

Now he had another whole day to kill. At least if he was in Chicago, he could drop in on Rick. Maybe invite his dad to brunch. He needed to shore up those long-neglected relationships. And either of those options would have been a far better use of his time than moping around Oak Hill.

But it was too late for second thoughts. He'd just have to make the best of the situation.

Lifting the lace curtain higher, he noted that the sun was trying to break through the heavy gray clouds. He could always head out to the countryside and take in the last burst of vibrant fall color the locals kept raving about. He'd never been much of a leaf watcher, but anything beat hibernating in his room.

A few minutes later, dressed in jeans and a black nylon Windbreaker, Mark descended the oak steps to find Marge in the inn's foyer. Attired in vibrant purple pants and a gauzy beaded tunic, she looked up at him as she slipped her arms into a coat.

"Morning, Mark. Coffee's on the sideboard in the dining room. Help yourself."

"Thanks."

"Any special plans for the day?"

"I thought I'd take a drive in the country."

"Not the best weather for that kind of thing." She gave him a skeptical look as she shrugged the coat onto her shoulders and reached for her purse.

"Any other suggestions?"

"We're having our monthly pancake breakfast at church. Best flapjacks this side of Harvey's Diner in Rolla. And served with homemade sausage. Can't beat it for the price. Everyone in town goes."

A church social. A few weeks ago, the very notion would have been ludicrous. The fact that he was actually considering the invitation showed how much his attitude had changed. Or just how bored he was. He wasn't sure which.

Before he could respond, Marge continued. "It wouldn't be like you're a stranger. You know Reverend Andrews. And the boys on the basketball team. Lots of folks from the *Gazette* are members of the congregation, too. Including Abby. She's working at the breakfast this morning."

"Abby will be there?"

Marge gave him a shrewd look. "That's right."

"What time?"

"Service is at nine. Breakfast will start about ten, ten-thirty. You're welcome to come to the service, too."

"I'm not quite dressed for that."

"You're in the country, Mark. You'll see everything from overalls and jeans to suits and ties. God doesn't have a dress code."

A smile tugged at his lips. "I'll think about it."

"You do that." She grabbed an umbrella from the ornate stand by the front door. "But don't think too hard. Sometimes it's better to listen to this—" she placed her hand over her heart "—than this," she finished by tapping her head.

Half an hour later, wedged into a pew in the very back of the church where he and Reverend Andrews had sat, Mark wasn't quite sure how he'd ended up there. It hadn't been a conscious decision. It had just...happened. One minute he'd been driving through the streets of the town, the next he'd been pulling into the lone vacant spot on the church parking lot where he'd coached the boys' basketball team before cooler weather had forced them indoors.

For several minutes he'd sat there, undecided. The sound of the organ, accompanied by a chorus of united voices, had drifted through the autumn air, beckoning him.

But considering his long estrangement from God, he'd hesitated, sure he would feel almost like an impostor if he joined that faithful group. Even though he was trying to work through his anger toward the Lord and lay to rest the sorrow and sense of loss that had colored his days for too many years, his issues were far from resolved. Yes, he'd taken a first, tentative step by sharing his feelings with Reverend Andrews. But he had a long way to go.

On the other hand, the minister had assured him that he wasn't alone in his imperfections. As a result, Mark felt confident that the man would welcome him to his flock.

Then there was Abby. She was inside those white-washed walls. That tugged at him, too—though going to church because he was attracted to a member of the congregation didn't seem like the noblest motivation.

Go or stay. Mark wrestled with the dilemma.

In the end, Mark stopped trying to analyze his decision and took Marge's advice. He followed his heart.

And he wasn't sorry. Though the place was crowded

and the service was well under way when he ventured into the back door, several people squeezed together to create a place for him, motioning for him to join them. Mark did his best to slip into the spot without attracting notice, but as he took his seat, Reverend Andrews glanced his way from the sanctuary. The smile he gave Mark chased away any lingering doubts about his welcome, and he acknowledged the minister with a discreet nod.

To his surprise, the hymns and prayers and readings from the Bible called up happy memories for Mark. Long ago, before Bobby and his mother died, he remembered attending church with his parents and Rick. It had been a larger and grander edifice than this, but the spirit had been the same. Then, as now, a sense of unity, of belonging, had pervaded the walls. In that place, surrounded by fellow believers, Mark had always felt closer to God, had sensed His love in a special way as it was made manifest in his believers. He felt that again now. And only then realized what a great void its absence had left in his life.

"Recall the words of Matthew. 'For where two or three are gathered together for my sake, there am I in the midst of them.'" Reverend Andrews had moved to the pulpit and launched into his sermon, and Mark tried to rein in his wayward thoughts and pick up the thread of the minister's message after missing the opening. "That's why we assemble here each Sunday—to feel the power of the spirit, to give witness to the world that we believe, to proclaim our faith and our trust in the Lord.

"But for that community witness to be strong, we

also need to know the Lord in a more personal way. To do that, we have to invest time and energy, just as we invest time and energy in developing other skills, such as shooting baskets or playing the piano or listening with an open, empathetic heart. All of those things take patience and practice and commitment to master."

Pausing, he let his gaze sweep over the congregation. "But I submit to you that the satisfaction that comes from refining those skills, worthy though they may be, can never match the satisfaction and peace and joy we receive when we make the effort to establish a personal relationships with the Lord and follow His call—no matter the surprising directions it can lead. Our private bond with Him is what gives this gathering meaning. Sunday worship is a joyful celebration of our individual relationships with the Lord and the power of our collective witness.

"My dear friends, coming to church is easy. Living our faith is hard. Both are important. But let us remember that when we leave here today, the Lord goes with us. Our faith is not in these four walls, but in the spirit living within us. As we go about our everyday lives, let's remember that the Lord walks with us not only on Sunday but on every day of the week. May we live accordingly so that we don't disappoint Him.

"Now let us pray…."

As the service continued, Mark bowed his head. He supposed he'd disappointed the Lord. Yet he'd been disappointed, too. In fact, disappointment had been his constant companion for more years than he cared to recall. Since he'd turned his back on the Lord, nothing in his experience had had the power to uplift him, to motivate him, to fill his life with joy and contentment. Everything fell short.

As a result, he'd lowered his expectations. And he'd erected a thick shell of bitterness around his heart. After Bobby and his mother died, that shell had protected him from further hurt. But it had also insulated his heart from love—and the healing grace of God.

All these years, Mark had lived on the surface of life, a day at a time, never counting on anything or permitting himself to be counted on. Enjoy the pleasures of the moment, shallow though they may be, and don't worry about tomorrow. Those had been the principles that guided his life.

Yet, in retrospect, he realized that he hadn't really enjoyed the so-called pleasures of his glitzy lifestyle. The many women he'd spent time with had provided fleeting gratification, but left him feeling emptier than ever. The liquor had mellowed his restlessness and ennui for brief intervals but only intensified the void in his life once the intoxication wore off. The travel and parties and trips to the health club had been mere diversions, designed to keep him busy and to distract him from the cold truth of his aimless, drifting life. A life that lacked purpose and direction and meaning.

A life that lacked God.

In turning away from his faith, Mark realized, he'd turned away from the one thing that could have stabilized his world and given it meaning in the midst of chaos. Because he'd demanded answers when there were none—or none that he could understand, as Reverend Andrews had pointed out—his quest had been doomed to failure. He'd put God to the test—and, in his mind, God had failed.

But he was the one who had failed, Mark acknowledged. By not putting his trust in God, by not placing his anguish in God's hands, he'd turned away from the one true source of consolation. That had been his big mistake.

And he'd been paying for it ever since.

Mark still didn't know how to go about mending the rift he'd created with the Almighty. But here, in this place, surrounded by people of faith, he found the courage to reopen a dialogue.

Please forgive me for turning away from You, Lord. I wish someone like Reverend Andrews had come into my life a long time ago so that I wouldn't have wasted all these years. But maybe I needed the years of emptiness to appreciate the things in life that really matter.

It's been a long journey, Lord. But like the prodigal son, I'd like to come home now. I ask You to show me the way. I suspect You've already set me on the right path by bringing me to Oak Hill. I ask that You give me the wisdom to discern Your will and the courage to follow Your direction—even if it leads in the surprising directions that Reverend Andrews mentioned today.

And, Lord...if Abby is part of Your plan for me, show me how to help her find a way to overcome the obstacles she's putting between us. Because I sense that they're formidable—and without Your intervention, perhaps insurmountable.

* * *

"This is a very generous gesture, Mark."

With a shrug, Mark stuck his hands in the pockets of his slacks as the minister stared, dumbfounded, at the sizeable check Mark had handed to him after the service. "I know there are a lot of Evans out there. And a lot of families like the Langes. I'm working on an idea that could help more of them. But in the meantime, this should smooth things out a bit for the Langes and give Evan his dream back." Mark did a quick survey of the church hall, where members of the congregation had gathered to enjoy their pancakes. "But remember—I want it kept anonymous."

"No problem. I'll say this came from a benefactor who didn't want to be identified." He pocketed the check with care. "I must admit I'm also intrigued about this idea you referred to."

"It's still in the proposal stage. But you'll be one of the first to know if anything comes of it."

"Then I'll be praying for good news. It sounds like a worthy initiative. Now why don't you have some pancakes? I see Marge over there waving. Looks like she saved you a place."

Turning, Mark grinned as the innkeeper pantomimed an invitation. Considering all the gray hair at her table, it looked like a meeting of the senior women's club.

"Go ahead. Make their day," the minister encouraged with a chuckle. "It's not every Sunday the ladies get to enjoy the company of a handsome young man. Meanwhile, I'll put this to good use." He patted his pocket and inclined his head toward a table in the far corner, where Evan sat with his family. "And I guarantee you'll make their day, too."

As the minister headed off, Mark worked his way toward Marge, scanning the hall as he edged around the packed tables. According to the minister, he'd already brightened several people's day. That left just one unresolved question.

Could he do the same for a certain newspaper editor?

What in the world was Mark doing at the pancake breakfast?

Stunned, Abby paused as she carried plates from the kitchen to the serving counter in the church hall. At least she thought it was Mark. She only had a back view of the tall man talking with Reverend Andrews. No, she had to be mistaken. This wasn't his kind of thing.

Then he turned his head and she got a good look at his strong, handsome profile. It *was* him! Her breath hitched in her throat and her pulse tripped into a staccato beat, destroying the calm she'd managed to create yesterday while hibernating at home to nurse the bruised knee she'd sustained in the collision. Once, a whole hour had gone by without thoughts of Mark flitting through her mind. But all he had to do was show up, and—wham!—she was reduced to a mass of quivering nerves and unruly yearnings.

Depositing the plates on the counter, Abby beat a hasty retreat to the safety of the kitchen and tried to think of an excuse to cut out early. But that wouldn't be fair to the breakfast committee. Besides, even if she ran away from the man, she couldn't run away from her feelings.

The pancake breakfast duty was so routine to her by now that she shifted into autopilot as she worked, leaving her mind free to think about the odd turn of events in her life during the past few months.

First, she'd been forced to accept the harsh reality that the *Gazette* wasn't going to survive without outside help, as well as the fact that in giving the paper the help it needed, she would be signing the death warrant for a family tradition. Even now, with Mark ensconced in the office, she was struggling to accept the bitter truth. Not to mention trying to come to grips with a life suddenly adrift and directionless. For as long as she could remember, she'd been certain of her path. But her route had been changed, and she had no map for the rest of her journey. It was an unsettling situation, to say the least.

As if that wasn't enough, Mark had added more turmoil to her life. Never in a million years had she expected to fall for the stuck-up, lazy playboy she'd talked with back in August. And she wouldn't have, if he'd lived down to her expectations. Instead, he'd surprised her by proving to be a hardworking, caring person. A person she could admire and respect.

A person she could love.

Closing her eyes, Abby drew a shaky breath. This was so wrong. His life was in Chicago. Hers was here. He was rich. She wasn't. He wore designer clothes. She'd been known to supplement her wardrobe at the thrift store in Rolla. He was sophisticated. She was the girl next door. It could never work. She had to fight this attraction.

But that task was formidable. She was pretty sure she

could manage it if the attraction was one-sided. Unfortunately, Mark seemed to return her feelings. And he also seemed determined to do something about it. There had been instances in the past couple of weeks when she'd seen tenderness and caring in his eyes, when he'd touched her with a gentleness and propriety that went beyond mere friendship. She suspected that all he needed was a little encouragement.

But she couldn't give him that. She had to be strong.

Fortified with new resolve, Abby balanced the next three plates on her arm, pushed through the swinging door into the serving area—and came face-to-face with Mark.

The slow smile that started at his lips and lit a fire in his eyes snatched away her resolve as easily as the capricious early-November breeze was plucking the leaves off the stately oak trees that lined her street.

"Hi." His voice was husky—and oh-so-appealing.

Abby refused to look at him, setting the plates on the serving counter with more care than necessary as she prepared to bolt. "This is a surprise. What are you doing here?"

"Having breakfast. Marge suggested it when I was at loose ends this morning. She invited me to the service, too."

"Did you come?" Abby stared at him, dumbfounded.

"Yes. I didn't see you up there, though."

"I went to the early service."

"That explains it, then. Reverend Andrews gave a great sermon, didn't he?" Reaching for a plate of pancakes, Mark grinned. "When do you get off?"

"After everyone is served."

"Any plans for this afternoon? I was going to take a drive in the country and I'd welcome some company."

He was asking her out! A delicious tingle ran up her spine, and waves of happiness lapped at her heart. She wanted to go. More than she could remember wanting anything in a very long time. The temptation to accept was almost too strong to fight.

But somehow she managed to summon up the self-discipline to refuse. "I have a bunch of things I need to take care of today. Thanks, anyway." With that, she turned and almost ran back into the kitchen.

Juggling his plate of pancakes and a cup of orange juice, Mark watched her go. He'd seen the yearning in her eyes, knew she'd wanted to accept his invitation. But she was obviously determined to maintain a distance between them.

Though he was disappointed, Mark wasn't giving up. She might have won the battle today. But when it came to determination, she'd met her match.

Chapter Twelve

"Mark! Can I ask you a favor?"

Turning, Mark saw Marge bustling toward him across the foyer of the inn. "Sure."

"Could you drop this off at Abby's house on your way to dinner? I meant to give it to her yesterday at church, but it slipped my mind. I try to get the minutes from the Chamber of Commerce board meetings to the members within a week, and I'm already a bit late this month."

Why was he not surprised that Abby served on the Chamber board? He'd already concluded that she was a human dynamo. Reaching for the envelope, he tucked it inside his leather jacket to protect it from the persistent rain. "No problem."

"Enjoy your dinner."

"Yeah. Thanks." The one thing he wouldn't miss when he left Oak Hill was the cuisine, he thought with a grimace as he dashed for his car through the cold drizzle. Delaying his meal for a few minutes was no sacrifice. Especially if it meant he could see Abby. She might be able to avoid him at the office, as she had all day today, but she couldn't very well ignore him if he was standing on her front porch.

Then again, maybe she could, he concluded a few minutes later, after ringing her bell twice and then resorting to the brass knocker without a response. Stifling his disappointment, he was starting to turn away when the sound of a crying baby made him freeze. A moment later, he heard a doorknob being turned, and the door swung open.

A few beats of silence ticked by as Mark took in the scene before him. Abby, dressed in a T-shirt and worn jeans, was juggling a blond, blue-eyed infant on her hip. She looked frazzled as she bounced the wailing baby, murmuring soothing sounds that didn't seem to be having any impact. Fat tears coursed down the child's face, and he—or she—had a death grip on Abby's T-shirt, its tiny fists bunching up the fabric.

So distracted was she by the baby that, for once, Mark's presence didn't seem to discombobulate her.

"Marge asked me to deliver the Chamber board meeting minutes on my way to dinner." Mark unzipped his jacket and withdrew the envelope, pitching his voice to be heard over the howls of the baby.

"Oh. Thanks. I was wondering..." A loud beep sounded from somewhere in the recesses of the house, and Abby gave him a flustered look. "I have to take a casserole out of the oven. Look, just come in for a minute, okay?"

Before she had a chance to rescind the invitation,

Mark retracted the envelope and stepped into the living room. Abby hesitated for an instant, as if the notion of Mark in her home unnerved her. Then she turned toward the kitchen. "I'll be right back."

Instead of waiting, Mark trailed after her through the small, simply furnished living room, noting with a frown that she was limping.

As he paused on the threshold, Abby made a valiant effort to settle the baby into a high chair beside the worn oak table in the homey kitchen. But the child would have none of it, tightening its grip on her shirt. The beep sounded again and, in desperation, Abby moved toward Mark and thrust the child into his arms.

Taken aback, Mark reacted on instinct and reached for the little noisemaker, depositing the envelope on the dinette table beside him. To his surprise, the baby released its grip on Abby, threw its arms around his neck, closed its mouth and rested its head on his shoulder. Quiet descended on the kitchen except for an occasional snuffle from the infant.

Considering that the only baby he'd held in his life was his niece, Elizabeth—and just on a couple of occasions, when she'd been forced upon him by his brother or Allison—he couldn't have been more surprised by the child's reaction. Nor, it seemed, could Abby, judging by her astonished expression.

Another high-pitched beep shattered the silence, and Abby turned, grabbed some pot holders and withdrew a savory-smelling casserole from the oven. Mark realized he'd give a week's salary for a few bites of whatever was in that glass dish.

When Abby looked at him again, she'd wiped the astounded look off her face. "You have quite a way with babies."

Glancing down, Mark saw that the infant in his arms had fallen asleep, its cheek nestled against his chest. A pleasing sensation tugged at his heart as he took in the sweeping lashes, the porcelain skin, the peaceful demeanor, the utter trust this fragile little creature had exhibited for a stranger. "I have no idea why."

"Some people have the knack. I don't always have good luck with her."

All at once, Mark began to put two and two together. Abby had come to the door holding a baby. The kitchen seemed well-equipped to handle an infant, with a high chair at the table and a playpen in one corner of the room. Jars of baby food were lined up on the counter. He stared at her. "You have a baby?"

She gave a startled burst of laughter. "Of course not. I'm not married."

So much for trying to add things up. He was going to have to dump his mathematical way of thinking one of these days. "That's not a requirement for parenthood these days," he defended himself.

Her smile faded, and the look she gave him was steady and direct. "It is for me."

Her response didn't surprise him. Abby was definitely the husband-and-two-kids-and-white-picket-fence type.

And maybe that was why she was putting up barriers between them, he suddenly realized. Considering all the messages Molly had taken for him from any number of women, Abby must have heard about his wide circle of female acquaintances. Perhaps she thought he was just looking for a little diversion in Oak Hill, a quick fling, a passing dalliance. Someone to pass the time with until he could return to his numerous companions in Chicago. And she wasn't the type to find that appealing.

Truth be told, neither was he. At least not anymore.

Yet…where did that leave him with her? Did he want a deeper relationship? And if he did, how would they manage to sustain it, with him returning to Chicago in a couple of weeks and Abby's roots firmly planted in Oak Hill?

He hadn't thought that far ahead. But he needed to. The last thing in the world he wanted to do was hurt Abby. Until he sorted through his intentions, a change of subject seemed in order.

"So who is this?" he asked, inclining his head toward the dozing baby.

"Caitlin. She and her mother live up the street. Linda's going to night school to get a nursing degree, and I watch Caitlin for her when her regular sitter is busy. Caitlin's daddy is in the service, stationed in the Middle East."

A sudden sensation of wetness caught Mark's attention, and he shifted the baby a bit to check it out. A spreading expanse of dampness was darkening the front of his oxford blue designer shirt. "I think she's leaking." He flicked a wry grin at Abby.

The look of horror on her face was almost comical. "One of the tabs on her diaper must have come loose." She moved forward and held out her arms. "I'll change her."

"No sense both of us getting wet. Where do you want her?"

After a brief hesitation, Abby nodded toward the living room. "On the floor in there." Grabbing a protective mat, she led the way—her limp more pronounced now. And she had difficulty lowering herself to the floor. The angry red burn on her forehead was the only visible sign of her accident three days before, but it appeared she'd sustained another injury, as well.

Dropping down beside her as she spread out the mat, Mark laid the baby on the waterproof square. "What's wrong with your leg?"

Her hand stilled for a brief instant as she dug through the diaper bag, then she continued her task. "I bruised my knee in the accident."

"It might be a good idea to have it checked out."

"I'll be fine. You can clean off your shirt in the bathroom down the hall. There are extra washcloths in the vanity."

Taking the hint to drop the subject, Mark followed her directions to the bathroom, located a washcloth and removed his jacket to scrub at his shirt.

She was taping the new diaper closed when he reappeared. As she reached for the baby, he restrained her.

"I'll take care of her in a minute. Let's get you up first."

Without giving her a chance to respond, he tossed his jacket onto a nearby chair and grasped her hands, easing her to her feet. He didn't miss the wince she tried to suppress as she put her weight on her leg.

"Are you sure you're okay?"

She looked up at him, a whisper away, his strong arms

supporting her, his warm brown eyes filled with concern—along with some other emotion she shied away from identifying. No, she wasn't okay. More than anything in the world she wanted to step into this man's embrace.

Fighting off that dangerous impulse, she managed to croak out a single word. "Yes."

After a brief hesitation, Mark released her and picked up Caitlin. Already the baby was drifting back to sleep. "Shall I put her in the playpen?"

"Yes. Thanks."

Back in the kitchen, Mark carefully lowered the sleeping baby into the portable crib and covered her with a blanket. She emitted a tiny sigh but didn't stir.

As Abby watched Mark's gentle ministrations to the infant, her throat tightened with emotion. The juxtaposition of his strong, capable, masculine fingers with the downy softness of the baby's fine, wispy hair and the pink fuzzy blanket pulled at some place deep inside her. Filled her with longing for a husband and a child of her own, a desire to create a warm, loving home where moments like these were the rule rather than the exception. A home where more than work gave her life meaning and joy. And perhaps someday she'd have that. But it wouldn't be with this man, she acknowledged with a pang.

When Mark turned toward Abby, her soft, wistful eyes reached deep into his heart. Before he could stop himself, he took a step forward. "Abby, I…"

"Y-you had an envelope for me from Marge?" Alarm sharpened her features, and she scooted back.

"Yeah." He picked it up from the table and handed

it over. When she took it, he noted that her fingers were trembling.

"Thanks. Sorry to delay your dinner."

"I'm eating at Gus's. Trust me, I'm in no hurry. The man only knows one cooking method—fried. I've ingested enough grease since I've been here to lube a car."

"I'm sure you could convince Marge to fix you a meal." A faint smile tugged at the corners of her mouth.

"I've tried that. I've now consumed my lifetime allotment of tofu." He cast a hopeful glance toward the casserole on the counter. "I'm open to a better offer. Price is no object."

Surprise registered on her face, followed by apology. "That's for the Langes. For tomorrow night."

"Ah." He swallowed past his disappointment. "Well, it was worth a try. I guess it's off to Gus's. Or Grease's, as I like to call it."

A niggle of guilt tugged at her conscience, reminding Abby that this man had come to her rescue on more than one occasion. Plus, he'd made a special trip over here tonight to deliver the board minutes. She ought to feed him. But it was hard enough to rein in the attraction between them in public. She feared it would be a losing battle in her own house.

As the seconds ticked by, she debated her decision. The right thing to do was ask him to stay. The smart thing to do was send him on his way. Should she follow her heart or let logic rule?

In the end, she was saved by the doorbell. But as Abby went to answer it, she knew that the interruption was just a reprieve. She still had a decision to make.

And she hoped that neither would live to regret it—whichever way it went.

"Dale! What a surprise! Come in."

As Abby stepped back to allow the sheriff to enter, she sensed that Mark had moved into the kitchen doorway behind her. Dale's surprised glance over her shoulder confirmed her suspicion—as did his greeting.

"Mark."

"Sheriff."

"Make it Dale." The lawman continued to appraise Abby's visitor for a moment, then turned his attention back to her. "I have some good news. We have a suspect in custody for the fire at Ali's restaurant and the various pranks that were directed at you. He's also been charged with some similar incidents in neighboring towns."

Relief coursed through Abby, easing the knot of tension in her stomach. "That's great! Can I offer you a soda while you fill us in?"

"No. I can't stay. I need to pick up Jenna at my mom's. But I thought you'd want to know right away."

"Who is it?" Mark moved behind Abby in a propriety stance the other man couldn't miss.

"Lee Callahan. Seventeen years old. Lives in Jasper Springs. His father was killed in the Middle East six months ago while serving a final tour of duty with the Marines. The kid's been unstable ever since. We got our first tip after that incident in Crandall. He had a little too much to drink at a party and started hinting that he had inside information about it. One of the kids who heard the story got scared and told his parents, and they called the police. It didn't take long after that."

"What will happen to him?" Concern etched Abby's features.

"It could be handled as a juvenile case. Or he could be tried as an adult. I expect the courts will take the circumstances into consideration when they make that call. And they'll get him some counseling." Dale checked his watch. "I've got to run. Depending on how things go with Lee, I may need you to fill out some paperwork, Abby. But at least you're safe now. Have a good evening, folks."

As she shut the door behind Dale and turned back to the room, Abby wasn't sure about the safe part. The hate-crimes incident might be behind them, but another threat stood across the room. Reminding her that she still hadn't decided whether or not to invite him to dinner.

"I'd offer to take you to Gus's to celebrate the good news if I didn't think it would do serious damage to your arteries." One corner of Mark's mouth quirked up. "Besides, you've probably had dinner already."

He'd given her an out, Abby realized. If she said she'd eaten earlier, she'd be off the hook and could send him on his way.

Except she hadn't. And she didn't want to send him away. Besides, what could it hurt to share one meal? It wasn't as if she was making a lifetime commitment. After the stress of the hate-crimes situation, didn't she deserve to celebrate the resolution?

Without giving herself a chance to debate further, Abby made her decision.

"I was too busy feeding the baby earlier. I'm going to eat now. You can join me if you like. Though I can't promise a very exciting menu. My diet is rather restricted."

Mark's smile warmed her all the way from the tip of her toes to the top of her head. "I'd love to. And anything is better than Gus's."

An hour later, as he polished off the last bites of a chicken breast seasoned with basil and oregano, brown rice and green beans amandine, Mark gave a satisfied sigh. "That was fabulous."

"You're easy to please. It can't compare to Cara Martin's fare at the Oak Hill Inn."

"She's good, I'll give you that. I'd pit her food against the best chefs in Chicago with no qualms. But that's more like a special occasion place. I like simpler meals on an everyday basis."

"Good, because simple is all you'll get with me. I have to work within the dietary restrictions dictated by my condition. Would you like some angel food cake for dessert? And coffee?"

"I thought diabetics couldn't eat sugar."

"That's a common fallacy. It's not so much what you eat as the total amount of carbohydrates you consume. As long as I balance out my starches, I can eat a little sugar once in a while."

"Then, by all means, I'd love some cake and coffee." Mark watched as Abby stood and moved about the small kitchen. Her tension at the beginning of the meal had been almost palpable, and he'd gone out of his way to put her at ease, keeping the conversation general. Now that she was a bit more relaxed, he felt comfortable edging toward more personal ground.

"You know, I mentioned that day you were jogging that I didn't know much about diabetes. But I've been doing some research on the Internet and I've learned a lot. Do you have to take insulin?"

"No. That's mostly for type 1 diabetes. Type 2 can often be controlled with diet and exercise alone. Some patients also need to take medication."

"So no shots?"

"No. Not yet, anyway." She cut a slice of cake and reached for another plate.

"Meaning that could be coming?"

"It's possible. That's what happened to my mother."

"She had diabetes, too?"

"Yes. You probably learned from your research that it can run in families. Hers started as type 2, but after a few years she developed what's called beta-cell failure. That means her pancreas stopped releasing insulin in response to high blood-sugar levels. After that, she needed the shots." Setting their cake and coffee on the table, Abby leaned down to check on Caitlin, her touch gentle and tender as she rearranged the blanket over the infant in the portable crib.

As he sipped his coffee, Mark considered how to proceed. He knew he needed to move slowly with Abby while he mulled over what level of commitment he was willing to offer, yet he wanted to get a handle on the obstacles that had spooked her. Until he knew what they were, he had no idea how—or if—they could be breached.

"She's a cute little thing." He glanced down at the sleeping baby beside the table. "Any nieces or nephews?"

"No. My brother is single—and not apt to get married in the foreseeable future."

"Why not?"

"He's got three years left on a five-year missionary commitment in Bolivia. The living conditions are primitive, and the work is demanding and exhausting. There's no opportunity—let alone energy—for romance." A brief flash of concern shadowed her eyes before she banished it. "But it's where he wants to be. Or, more importantly, where he believes God wants him to be. I miss him a lot, though. We've always been friends as well as siblings, despite the fact that he's four years older than me."

"I have a brother, too. Younger by five years. He's married and has a five-year-old daughter. They live in Chicago."

"How nice. You must get to see them often."

"No. Unlike you and your brother, we've never been close. My fault, not his. He's tried to keep in touch, but I never reciprocated."

"Why not, if you don't mind me asking?" Abby sent him a curious look over the rim of her cup as she raised it to her lips.

Unsure how to respond without getting into a discussion of the whole complicated mess he'd made of his life, Mark hesitated. He could brush off her question and let the matter drop. But if he wanted to change, if he wanted to start allowing people in, he had to learn to open up. Maybe now was the time to start. Or at least take the first tentative steps.

"I have a hard time letting people get close. When I was thirteen, I lost my best friend and my mother just months apart. My friend to leukemia, and my mother to a cerebral hemorrhage," he said quietly. To his surprise, he found the words easier to say than he'd expected. Perhaps because he'd already shared his story with Reverend Andrews.

"After they died, I shut down. I didn't want to get hurt again by letting myself care for someone, only to lose them, too. I also turned my back on God. But thanks to a number of things that have happened in the past few weeks, I realize that was a mistake. And I'm trying to rectify it. I want a richer, fuller, more meaningful life. Even if that entails risk."

Stunned—and touched—by the raw honesty of his revelation, Abby had to fight down the impulse to take his hand in a comforting clasp.

"I'm sorry for all you've been through." She tightened her fingers around her mug—the only way to ensure that her hands behaved. "But I'm glad you're finding your way out of that darkness. Shutting people out can make for a very lonely existence."

"Speaking of shutting people out, may I ask you something, Abby?"

Uh-oh. She knew where this was heading. And she didn't want to go there.

Sensing her withdrawal, Mark plunged ahead, anyway. "I've been wondering why you haven't married. Unlike me, you don't seem to have a problem with commitment. You have a warm and caring heart, and I can see that you love children. I don't understand why you're still single."

Abby fiddled with her coffee cup. "The *Gazette* has always been my passion. It hasn't left me much time or energy for romance. Besides, we don't exactly have an abundance of eligible men in Oak Hill."

"There's one here now."

At his candid comeback, Abby shot him a startled look. If ever she'd harbored any doubts about his interest, his tender expression dispelled them. She had to wait for her lungs to reinflate before she could speak. "I'm not in the market for a relationship, Mark."

"With me—or with anyone?"

She swallowed. He'd been honest with her about his interest; she was left with no choice but to be honest in her response. "With you."

As he scrutinized her, he tried to make sense of her answer. He knew she was attracted to him, that she felt the chemistry between them. He'd dated enough women to recognize the signs. That wasn't the problem.

"Is it because of Campbell Publishing's interest in the *Gazette?*"

"No."

"Then what?"

Instead of responding, she stood and moved toward the sink, turning away from him. Once there, she gripped the porcelain edge, her shoulders rigid, her head bowed. Even from across the room, Mark could sense her distress, knew she was struggling for control.

Scraping back his chair, he rose and moved behind

her. She went still as he approached, stiffening when he rested his hands lightly on her slight shoulders. Beneath his fingers he could feel her trembling, though her muscles were as taut and unyielding as the synthetic leather on the basketball he'd bought at the local hardware store.

"Abby…I'm sorry. I didn't mean to upset you."

His soft, concerned voice close to her ear, his warm breath on her cheek, the gentle touch of his hands, threatened her shaky control.

"You need to go, Mark. Now," she choked out.

Ignoring her plea, he exerted pressure on her shoulders, urging her to turn toward him. She resisted, averting her face, but his glimpse of the silent tears coursing down her cheeks jolted him. He was used to Abby being strong and in control. This side of her tore at his gut. *Lord, help me deal with this,* he pleaded in a prayer born of desperation. *I'm way out of my depth here.*

"Why?" he asked softly. Cupping her face with his hands, he angled it toward him and wiped away her tears with his thumbs, searching her troubled eyes for an answer. "I don't understand."

"It wouldn't work between us."

"Because of my past?" He hated to bring it up, hated to even remember it, but he figured Abby suspected that he'd led a less-than-admirable life. For a woman like her, that could be a huge stumbling block. "If I could change it, I would. But all I can control is the future. And I can promise you my wild days are over."

"It's not that. I don't think it's fair to hold someone's

past against them when they're doing their best to create a better future."

"Okay." Relieved, he tried another tack. "Is it the long-distance issue?"

No response.

"Come on, Abby. Talk to me." He pried her cold hands off the edge of the sink and enfolded them in his warm clasp.

His gentle entreaty was hard to ignore. Yet Abby wasn't prepared for this discussion tonight. One peek at the resolute set of his lips, however, told her that he wasn't going to give up until he got an answer.

Staring at a button on his shirt, she bit her lip and took a deep breath. "We're too different."

Her reply was met with silence. When the silence lengthened, she risked a look at him. He seemed confused.

"That's it?"

"That's enough."

"I don't think we're that different. At least not anymore."

She tried to tug her hands free, but he refused to relinquish his grasp. "Uh-uh. We need to sort this out. What do you mean by *different?*"

"It's obvious."

"Not to me."

"Mark, think about our backgrounds." She lifted her chin and gave him an earnest look. "Small town, big city. Rich, not rich. Man of the world, girl next door. Cocktail parties with caviar, pancake breakfasts at church. We live in different worlds."

"Okay." He mulled that over. "But different

doesn't mean incompatible. And none of those differences are insurmountable. We can deal with them if things get serious."

"That's what my parents thought, too."

There was a world of pain in her response, and Mark knew that he'd at last gotten to the heart of her problem. He had a feeling it wouldn't be easy to convince her to share whatever unhappy memories stood in the way of their relationship, but he also knew that he had to succeed. Only when he found out what was holding her back would he know how to fight her fears.

"Tell me about them, Abby."

"It's a long story."

"I don't have to be anywhere tonight."

Abby looked up into Mark's warm brown eyes, torn. Her parents' unhappy marriage wasn't a topic she'd ever discussed with anyone. It had seemed disloyal to tell anyone else about the problems that they'd kept behind closed doors.

Now, however, she had a reason to drag those skeletons out of the closet. Like her parents, Mark seemed to think that love would be enough to overcome their differences.

But she knew better.

And it was time Mark did, too.

Chapter Thirteen

"Let's sit, okay?" Abby tugged her hands free, and this time Mark let her go. When he sat beside her a moment later, she stared at the worn oak table and traced the uneven grain with her finger.

"We always ate dinner together at this table. The four of us—my mom and dad and my brother and I."

"Are those good memories?" He wasn't sure how to interpret the tenor of her voice.

"Some are. Most aren't."

"Why not?"

"Too much tension."

Patience had never been one of his strengths, but he waited to see if she'd continue. After a few seconds, she did.

"Were your parents happy, Mark?"

Her wistful question took him off guard. "Yes. Very."

"Did your mom and dad have similar backgrounds?"

"Yes. They both came from middle-class families.

But Dad had great ambitions, and Mom believed in him. They were a good team."

"That makes a big difference."

"Are you saying that your mom didn't support your dad?"

"I think she did the best she could. She and Dad met when they were seniors in college and married a month after they graduated, and she knew Dad would eventually take over the family business. But she didn't have a clue what she was getting into when she came to live in Oak Hill. Mom was from a wealthy family in San Francisco. She loved art and theater and music. She was a gifted pianist, and I'm sure she would have been successful in her field of fashion design. But there wasn't much opportunity for her to pursue any of those things in Oak Hill."

"I take it she was unhappy here."

"Yes. At least as far back as I can remember." Abby turned away to check on Caitlin, envying the peaceful countenance of the slumbering infant. "But, to her credit, her disillusionment didn't keep her from being a good mother. She always took pride in our accomplishments, and she was never too busy to read my brother and me a bedtime story or take us outside to stargaze or spend hours with us looking for cloud pictures on warm summer days."

"It sounds like you loved her very much."

"I did. And I loved Dad, too. But he was also unhappy. He felt like he'd failed Mom. Yet, short of selling the business, there wasn't much he could do to change their circumstances. And that's never been an option for a Warner. The paper has always been a sacred trust passed from one generation to the next."

A shadow of distress darkened her features, and Mark took her cold hand in his. He was grateful that she didn't pull away.

"Anyway, it wasn't a happy marriage. They kept up a good front in public, but my brother and I were aware of the tension. They were just too different, Mark. Trying to meld two disparate worlds doesn't work."

"It can if both people are committed to making it work."

"I'm sure my parents believed that, too, when they married."

"But they were young, Abby. College kids. They fell in love in the rarified atmosphere of a campus. That's not real life. And they may not have thought through all the ramifications of their marriage. We're older than they were. I'm sure we both have a better handle now on what's important than we did in our college days. And a better sense of what commitment means—the benefits and the sacrifices."

She leveled a steady gaze at him. "You wouldn't want to live in Oak Hill full-time any more than I'd want to live in Chicago. How would we get around that?"

It was a fair question. And he didn't have a good answer. Yet. "If things got serious between us, there would have to be compromises on both sides. We'd have to figure that out."

It was a lame response and he knew it. Abby's hard-hitting comeback told him she did, too.

"I like you, Mark. A lot. But my future is in limbo. As far as I can see, yours is secure. When your job here is finished, you'll go back to your life in Chicago. Someday you'll take over your father's business. If we pursued a relationship, I'm the one who would have to uproot myself, leave the only home I've ever known and find something else to give my life meaning. That's not compromise, that's capitulation. And I could very well end up resenting you, like my mother resented my dad. Take it from one who knows, that's no way to live."

"I can see you've given this a lot of thought."

"I told you, Mark—I like you. I wish there was a way to guarantee a happy ending. But there isn't."

He gave her a speculative look. "Do you know what I think?"

"What?" Her expression was wary.

"I think we're thinking too much. To use an old cliché, we may be putting the cart before the horse. I've never even kissed you."

"Maybe that's just as well. It would only complicate things."

That's what he was counting on. Without responding, he stood and reached down, pulling her to her feet.

"What are you doing?" Surprise widened her eyes.

"Let's stop thinking for a few minutes. And talking." Before she could protest, he drew her close and wrapped his arms around her, tucking her head into his shoulder as he rested his chin on her soft, satiny hair.

"Mark, I don't think this…"

"No thinking for a minute, okay?"

She fell silent, and he stroked her back, aware of how well she fit into the protective circle of his arms. As if that was where she belonged. Though he'd been attracted to her for weeks, had fantasized about holding her in his arms, even his wildest imagination had never conjured up this sense of completeness.

Of rightness.

The feeling blew him away—and reaffirmed his conviction that they needed to explore the magnetism that had drawn them together. He hoped—prayed—that Abby would come to the same conclusion, despite her reservations, now that she was in his arms.

As Mark held her close, the evening stubble on his chin a bit scratchy—and appealing—as he rubbed it against her temple, Abby considered what he'd said. It was true that her parents had been young when they'd married. And it was possible they hadn't thought through the ramifications of their decision.

It was also true that she and Mark were older. They both knew what was important to them. And they were reasonable adults, used to negotiating. Might they be able to work out an arrangement that would allow both sides to avoid the resentment that had sabotaged her parents' marriage?

Drawing back a bit, Abby looked up at him. He dropped his hands to her waist but didn't break contact.

"It feels good in your arms," she said softly.

A slow smile warmed his face. "You feel good in my arms, too. Like I knew you would."

As Mark searched her eyes, he saw yearning spring to life in their depths. She wanted him to kiss her as much as he wanted to taste her lips. But she was uncertain. Wondering if it was wise.

Frankly, he had no idea. And at the moment he didn't much care.

Following the advice he'd given Abby, Mark stopped thinking and lowered his head to brush his lips against hers. Her sweet, artless response surprised him—and stirred him more than the practiced attentions of any of the sophisticated women he'd dated. When her arms crept around his neck, it took every ounce of his willpower to refrain from intensifying the embrace. Not tonight, he told himself. Tonight, this was enough.

When the gentle, exploratory kiss ended, she drew a shaky breath. "That felt good, too."

"I agree. Which goes to show that we're not as different as you seem to think we are."

"There's more to a relationship than kissing."

"It's a good start." He gave her an unrepentant grin. "And it can smooth out a lot of rough patches."

"Not in my parents' case."

His grin faded. It had been too much to hope that one kiss would wipe away her doubts. "But they stayed together, didn't they?"

"Yes. I'm not sure they would have long-term, though, if Mom hadn't died so young."

"How old was she?"

"Thirty-eight."

A frown creased Mark's brow. "I didn't realize that. What happened to her?"

"She had a low-blood-sugar episode in the middle of the night and slept through the early symptoms. When my father tried to wake her the next morning, she was already in a deep coma. She died later that day."

A muscle twitched in Mark's jaw and his mouth settled into a grim line. In all his research, he'd found nothing to suggest that sudden complications of that magnitude were common in diabetics. But he'd seen Abby in the throes of such an episode. Had witnessed the debilitating—and potentially life-threatening—nature of the attack. She'd assured him that day that they were rare, yet her mother had died from one. In her sleep.

"You're saying that diabetes killed your mother." It was more statement than question as he struggled to absorb Abby's bombshell.

"Yes. But she was never the most organized person. Dad had to constantly remind her about monitoring and medication and diet."

"Okay." He processed Abby's explanation, trying to fit all the pieces together. "But you had a dangerous episode, too. And you're very conscientious."

"I got distracted that day. Trust me, I learned my lesson. It won't happen again."

He wanted to believe her. Desperately. But she was human. And people made mistakes. What if he wasn't around the next time? The thought terrified him.

"I'm still adjusting to the disease, Mark." Abby touched his cheek. "And learning how to deal with it. I don't expect to have the problems my mom did."

"But you can't eliminate all the risks."

"No." If he was looking for absolute assurances, she couldn't give him any. Just as there were no guarantees that two people from different worlds could sustain a relationship long-term, neither was there a guarantee that they'd even *have* a long-term.

Feeling blindsided and stunned, Mark stared at Abby. For the first time in twenty-one years, he'd let himself care about someone else. But he'd already lost two people he loved to unforgiving medical conditions. Could he risk setting himself up for a third loss?

If this was God's way of testing his reawakening faith, he was failing, Mark acknowledged. How could he put his trust in a God who would bring him this far only to throw him such a malicious curve? If he gave his heart to this woman and then lost her, too, he'd never recover.

His gut clenched as he looked into Abby's deep green eyes. The kind of eyes a man could get lost in. Why couldn't she have been a normal, healthy woman? Someone he wouldn't have to worry about losing every day of his life? A few minutes ago he'd been sure that no problem between them was insurmountable. Now he wasn't as certain. Yet how could he walk away? He'd never met anyone like Abby. And he had a feeling he never would again.

As questions and doubts bombarded him, Mark felt like a sailor clinging to a mast in a raging storm—and who was fast losing his grip.

"Are you sure your mother didn't have other health issues that predisposed her to problems with the diabetes?" He was grasping at straws, looking for something that would reassure him about Abby's condition.

"Not that I know of. I'm pretty certain her problems were due to negligence." She blinked past a shimmer of tears. "Look, it might be best if we call it a night."

He didn't want to go. But he didn't belong here, either, he realized. Not until he sorted through his emotions. Regained his balance. A feat he would never accomplish as long as Abby stood in the circle of his arms, inches away, her sorrowful expression ripping his soul to shreds.

"I guess we have a lot to think about after all." It was the best he could offer tonight.

"I guess we do." Sadness nipped at the edges of her voice. For weeks she'd reined in her feelings, afraid to risk loving a man who came from such a different world. How ironic that tonight, just as she'd begun to consider taking that risk, he seemed to be having second thoughts about taking the risk of loving *her.*

In a triumph of will over desire, Mark took a step back. He needed to think this through. For both their sakes. "Good night, Abby." He lifted his hand toward her face. Let it drop. And without another word, he turned and walked out the door.

The gusty November wind buffeted him as he headed toward his car, churning the leaves around him in counterpoint to his roiling emotions as he, too, mulled over the irony of their situation.

He'd set out on a quest to convince her to take a chance on their relationship.

Yet in the end *he* was the one who didn't seem to have the stomach for risk.

Chapter Fourteen

Wiping a weary hand down his face, Mark pushed through the door of the *Gazette* into the lobby, bringing a gust of cold air with him. He'd slept little after the bombshell Abby had dropped the night before. Her mother had died at thirty-eight. Abby was thirty-two. How was he supposed to live with that?

He'd tried praying, but that hadn't offered him any consolation—or a solution. At least not yet. And he had no idea what he would say to her when they next met.

"Morning, Molly. Is Abby here yet?"

The receptionist spared him no more than a quick glance over her shoulder as she typed, his presence now routine at the newspaper. "Morning. No. She had a doctor's appointment."

Panic clutched at Mark's gut. "What's wrong with her?"

"She mentioned a problem with her knee." Molly gave him an odd look. "Are you okay? You look a little pale yourself."

It took him a few seconds to tame his racing pulse. "Yeah. I'm fine."

As he headed down the hall toward the conference room, the taste of fear sharp on his tongue, Mark thought about Abby's father. No wonder he'd died young of a heart attack.

Not that Mark was worried about the risk of a heart attack. Dying was easy. It was the prospect of living day after day with constant fear that knotted his stomach. But that's what he'd be dealing with if he got serious about Abby.

Once seated in the conference room, Mark rested his elbows on the table, linked his fingers and lowered his head.

Lord, I don't want to lose Abby, but I don't know how to deal with her illness. Or address the concerns she raised last night about the differences in our backgrounds. Please help me find some answers. Reverend Andrews said we should follow Your call—no matter the surprising directions it might lead. But I guess I didn't realize how frightening some of them could be. I ask two things of You in the days ahead. Wisdom to discern Your will for me—and the courage to follow it.

"It's a bad bruise, Abby. But I don't think there's any other damage. And it looks about the way it should a few days into the healing process." Dr. Martin probed her knee once more, then straightened up. "Keep an eye on it and take some aspirin to help with the discomfort. If it doesn't start to feel a lot better in the next couple of days, call me. How's everything else?" He took a seat on the stool in the examining room.

"Okay."

"That doesn't sound too convincing." He gave her an assessing look.

She tried to respond in a calm tone, but the words came out strained. "It's been a tough few weeks. Campbell Publishing is interested in acquiring the *Gazette*. The only alternative seems to be to let it die. Neither option is good."

"How are you handling the stress?"

"Fine."

His skepticism was obvious as he tapped his pen against her file. "Any medical problems you need to tell me about?"

She lowered her head and fiddled with the edge of the paper liner on the examining table. Like old Doc Adams, who'd retired a couple of years ago, Sam Martin was way too perceptive. "I did have a low-blood-sugar incident."

"When?"

"About a month ago."

"What happened?"

"I was distracted and I overdid my exercise. But I had candy with me."

"So you were able to get this under control on your own?"

She squirmed under his probing gaze. "Not exactly. It hit pretty fast, and I was jogging in the country. Mark Campbell happened to be driving by and he helped me."

"Have you discussed this with Dr. Sullivan?"

"No. I recovered quickly, and I haven't had any repercussions. I did monitor my glucose levels more often for the next few days, and everything was normal. I haven't had any further problems."

When he didn't respond at once, she looked up to find him frowning. She supposed she should have called her endocrinologist in St. Louis. It would have been the prudent thing to do. Hadn't she told Mark just last night that she was more responsible and diligent about taking care of herself than her mother had been?

"I want you to promise me that you'll discuss this with Dr. Sullivan. Today." Sam Martin pinned her with an intent look. "I know you have a lot on your mind with the paper, Abby, but your health needs to be a priority. How we treat this disease in the early stages could affect its development, and Dr. Sullivan will want to track every blip in your condition."

"Okay. I'll call him."

"Good." Dr. Martin went back to writing on her chart, and Abby focused on the network of scars that covered his right hand, the result of a traumatic injury that had forced him to give up surgery. At least her condition hadn't deprived her of the work she loved, she mused. Yet based on Mark's reaction to her mother's death, it could very well deprive her of an unexpected opportunity for love.

"Something else seems to be on your mind, Abby."

At Dr. Martin's astute observation, she managed to dredge up a smile. "Heart concerns. But not the kind the medical community can fix."

Empathy softened his features. "There's no prescription for that, I'm afraid. However, I'm happy to listen if you'd like to talk about it."

For a second, Abby was taken aback. In the past, Dr.

Martin had conducted his exams in a very methodical, clinical style that offered little opportunity for conversation. Since his reconciliation with his wife over the past summer, however, he'd adopted a holistic approach that warmed him up and prompted confidences. She decided to test the waters.

"There is one question you might be able to answer. But the whole situation is a bit complicated."

"Isn't it always?"

His rueful, understanding smile encouraged her to continue.

"The thing is, Mark and I have…we've gotten kind of close during this whole process. But all along I kept putting up barriers…for a lot of reasons. Then he found out about my mom dying at thirty-eight and freaked out. The lives of two people he loved were cut short by leukemia and a cerebral hemorrhage, and I think he's worried that could happen again.

"Anyway, he asked me the other night if my mom might have had any other medical issues that predisposed her to an early death from diabetes. As far as I know, she didn't. I always thought she died because she was careless about her care. I told that to Mark, but after witnessing my episode, I don't think he's convinced."

A slight frown creased Dr. Martin's brow. "I don't know the details of your mother's history, but I'm very familiar with your condition. And as long as you're diligent in your monitoring and checkups, I see no reason why you can't have a long and productive life. Nor is there any reason you can't marry or have a family. I'm sure Dr. Sullivan would concur."

"And you don't think there's anything in my mother's file to suggest she had other contributing problems?"

"I pulled it from our archives to review it when you were diagnosed, and I don't recall anything in particular. But I'll tell you what—let me do a little digging and I'll give you a call with what I find. Fair enough?"

"Are you sure you don't mind?"

"Not at all. I would hate for misinformation to stand in the way of romance." Rising, he moved toward the door, stopping on the threshold to look back at her. "I'll call you early next week. With good news, I expect. In the meantime, take care of yourself as well as the *Gazette.* We don't want that suitor of yours to get any more spooked than he already is." With a smile, he disappeared through the door.

As Abby stood and picked up her purse, she felt hopeful that Dr. Martin's research would allow her to allay Mark's concerns about her health.

As for her own concerns about their different backgrounds, there was no quick fix. Mark had made some good points last night. But if they decided to explore their attraction, there would have to be a lot of negotiation. And the situation was complicated by Abby's uncertainty about her future. Until the fate of the *Gazette* was decided, she was in limbo.

Meaning that whatever Dr. Martin discovered might help, but it wasn't going to solve all of their problems.

With a final blow on his whistle, Mark signaled the end of his last basketball practice. Jim Jackson had recovered enough to resume his duties—good timing, considering that Mark would be leaving Oak Hill in a matter of days. But he was going to miss his interaction with the boys. It had been satisfying to watch them develop from a clumsy tangle of arms and legs to a cohesive team with excellent potential.

Tonight's practice had also been a good stress reliever. Abby had kept her door shut since her doctor's visit, and he hadn't sought her out. He needed some space to think things through. Coaching the boys had given him a welcome mental break.

As the team members gathered around him in the school gym, he smiled. "Great job. Mr. Jackson will be proud of you. And I have no doubt that you'll be ready for your first real game in January. I also want to thank you for letting me work with you these past few weeks. It's been a terrific experience, and I know you guys are going to offer your competitors a real challenge. Good luck."

Mark started to turn away, but a murmur ran through the group, and he paused to find Evan shouldering his way forward. Since Mark had made his anonymous contribution to the church, earmarked for the Langes, Evan had seemed far more upbeat. In fact, in the past couple of practice sessions he had again lived up to the promise Mark had seen in him at the beginning. That was all the thanks Mark needed—or wanted—for his generosity. Nor did he expect anything in return for his coaching gig. But it appeared the team had other ideas.

As Evan approached, he held out a flat square

package topped with a blue bow. "This is from the guys, Mr. Campbell."

An odd tightness in Mark's throat rendered speech impossible. He took the gift, tore off the wrapping and lifted the lid of the box inside to find a plaque featuring the team emblem. The sentiment was simple—and heartfelt. "'With appreciation and gratitude to Mark Campbell for generously sharing his coaching expertise in our time of need. We'll never forget you.'" Each of the boys' names was inscribed.

For a long moment Mark held the plaque, struggling to contain his emotions. A few months ago, if someone had told him he'd be coaching a ragtag basketball team in the nation's heartland, he'd have laughed. Nor would he have believed that a simple gift like this would mean more to him than any of the expensive decorative items that filled his condo. But he had. And it did.

"Thank you, guys." He stopped and cleared his throat. "This means a lot. And I'll never forget you, either." He shook hands with each of them, then watched as the group dispersed. Only then did Reverend Andrews step forward.

"Were you behind this?" Mark lifted the plaque.

"I arranged to have it made. But it was their idea. And well-deserved. You did a good job with them, Mark. I wish we could keep you around." The man held out his hand. "I hope I see you again before you leave, but if not, thank you. And God go with you."

As Mark walked out the door a few minutes later, he prayed that God would heed the minister's prayer. He had a lot of issues to resolve in the next few days. And having God by his side couldn't hurt.

What was that noise?

Pulled from a deep, dreamless slumber, it took Mark a few seconds to identify the rapping sound that had disrupted his sleep. Someone was knocking on his door.

Squinting at his watch, Mark tried to focus. Not an easy task. Since Abby had dropped the news about her mother's death on him three days ago, sleep had been elusive. When he did drift off, exhaustion tended to impose a mind-numbing coma that was hard to shake. But at last the numbers came into focus. One o'clock in the morning.

"Mark? It's Marge. Are you awake?"

At the innkeeper's anxious tone, the last vestiges of sleep vanished. Nothing less than a serious problem would persuade her to wake up a guest in the middle of the night. Heart pounding, he threw back the covers and swung his legs to the floor, reaching for the jeans he'd tossed on a nearby chair.

"Yeah. I'm up. Give me a sec."

Shoving his feet into the denim, he smoothed back his hair with one hand and padded barefoot to the door. When he opened it, Marge stood on the other side, wearing some kind of psychedelic caftan that would have hurt his eyes if the dim illumination in the hallway had been any stronger. At any other time, he would have had to smother a grin. But her worried expression chased away any semblance of levity.

Bracing himself, he gripped the door frame. "What's wrong?"

"Your brother is on the phone. He says he tried your cell but the call wouldn't go through. You can take it in the parlor."

Allison. Something must be wrong with Allison. Or the baby. Mark didn't think Rick would call in the middle of the night to announce a normal delivery. With a clipped nod, Mark ran down the steps to the first floor, trying to rein in his pounding pulse as he snatched up the phone. "Rick? What's up? Is Allison okay?"

"Yes, she's fine. Sorry to bother you in the middle of the night, Mark. It's not Allison. It's Dad. He's had a stroke."

Mark sucked in a harsh breath. "How bad?"

"The doctors aren't sure yet. It seems pretty mild, but they won't know until they run a bunch of tests. He's not in any immediate danger, but I thought you'd want to know right away. Dad's secretary gave me the name of the place you're staying."

"Yeah. Listen…I'll head for St. Louis and grab the first flight I can get. What hospital?" Once he had the information, Mark took another look at his watch. "Depending on when I can get out, I think I can be there pretty early in the morning."

"Why don't you wait until daylight? It might be safer than driving the back roads when you're half-asleep."

He wasn't half-asleep anymore. Not by a long shot. "I'm fine. And I want to be there." The need to strengthen his ties with his long-neglected family had been building inside him for the past few weeks, but it hadn't seemed urgent. Now it did. Too bad it had taken a crisis to prompt him to action.

"Okay, if you're sure. I'll still be hanging out at the hospital."

As Mark rang off and headed for the stairs, he saw Marge waiting at the top.

"My father's had a stroke. I have to go back to Chicago right away."

"Of course. Leave everything you don't need in the room. Business is slow this time of year. I don't expect I'll need the space."

"Thanks."

"I'll fix you a thermos of coffee to take." She turned toward the steps and started down.

"You don't need to bother."

Pausing, she looked back at him. "It's no bother, Mark. That's what friends are for."

Mark didn't argue. He could use the coffee. And friends. Including a spiritual one he had also neglected for far too long.

As he threw a few necessities into an overnight bag, he took a moment to send a plea heavenward.

Lord, I know I've made a mess of things. But I'd like to change that. I think my priorities are finally getting straightened out. And I'm beginning to understand the importance of relationships—neglected ones and new ones. Please give me the chance to talk with Dad. I know he's been concerned about me and my lack of direction. I'd like to ease his mind on that score, at least.

But, whatever happens, help me stay the course I've started on. Because I don't want to fall back to the life I led before.

* * *

The cryptic message left at one-thirty in the morning was waiting for Abby when she arrived at work on Friday.

"Abby, it's Mark. I'm heading back to Chicago. My dad's had a stroke, and I'm planning to catch the next flight out from St. Louis. I'll be in touch."

Closing her eyes, Abby said a silent prayer for Spencer Campbell—and for his son. She'd been through her share of medical emergencies, knew all about the stomach-clenching fear that accompanied them. And Mark had experienced more than his quota, too.

The sudden ring of her phone startled her, and she grabbed for it.

"Abby? Sam Martin. Do you have a minute?"

"Yes." With an effort, she switched gears.

"I was able to pull your mother's file yesterday, and it's clear from Dr. Adams's notes that she wasn't the most diligent person when it came to taking care of herself. He recorded numerous hypoglycemic episodes that seem to be a function of neglect. According to his notes, she had one such incident the day before she died. I suspect she didn't regulate her blood-sugar as conscientiously as she should have prior to going to bed that night. As far as I can see, there's nothing to indicate she had any other conditions that would have exacerbated her diabetes."

"That's good news. Thank you for calling, doctor."

"My pleasure. Take care."

As Abby rang off, she let out a long, slow sigh of relief. That was one less hurdle to deal with in their relationship. Whether it solved Mark's issue with her health, however, remained to be seen. Bottom line, she still didn't come with any guarantees.

For now, though, she suspected their relationship was the last thing on his mind. Until Spencer Campbell's health was stable, Mark's father would be his top priority.

In the meantime, she would pray. For Spencer, of course. But also for guidance—and courage. For her *and* Mark. Once this crisis was resolved, they would have decisions to make. Ones that could change their lives forever. For better…or for worse.

And the potential for worse was precisely why they were both afraid.

Chapter Fifteen

Mark hated hospitals.

As he stepped off the elevator near the intensive care unit, the ubiquitous antiseptic smell seemed to permeate his brain, awakening old—and traumatic—memories. His mother hadn't been in the hospital long—mere hours. But he'd made enough trips during Bobby's illness for that scent to etch itself indelibly in his mind.

Inhaling it again now brought back all the pain and grief and fear he'd known more than twenty years ago. As did the sound of carts being wheeled down the hall and the relentless muted beeping from monitors within the shadowy rooms lining the long corridor.

His gut clenched, and Mark stopped to lean against the wall, closing his eyes as he took a slow, deep breath. Blindsided by the barrage of harrowing reminders from the past and the sudden rush of raw feeling, he felt ill equipped to deal with either. It took every bit of self-discipline he could muster to subdue the almost overpowering impulse to turn around, get back in the elevator and run away from this place.

That's what he'd done when Bobby died, he recalled. But even then, while he'd been able to physically distance himself from the reality, he hadn't been able to run from the emotional horror. Nor could he now. He had to face this.

"Mark? Are you okay?"

A steadying hand came down on his shoulder, and he opened his eyes to find Rick regarding him with concern. His brother's unshaven face was lined with weariness and worry, his eyes were bloodshot, his clothes rumpled.

Making a Herculean effort to stem the tide of painful emotions that threatened to swamp him, Mark straightened up. "I think I should ask *you* that question. You look like something the cat dragged in."

"To use another old cliché, that's like the pot calling the kettle black."

Mark didn't doubt that he looked as bad as Rick did after his midnight race through the dark Missouri countryside and his red-eye flight to Chicago. Reaching up, he rubbed the coarse stubble on his jaw. "I guess we're quite a pair. How long have you been here?"

"Since Dad was brought to the emergency room. About ten o'clock last night."

"How is he?"

"Stable. We'll know more when they finish the battery of tests they're running."

"Can I see him?"

"Sure. They're getting ready to take him down for

another scan, but you can catch him if you duck in real quick." He inclined his head toward a doorway. "I'll wait here."

As Mark entered the ICU, stepping over cords and skirting the flashing monitors, he checked out the room. None of the faces in the beds were familiar, but a few technicians and nurses were clustered in one curtained area. They parted as he headed in their direction, giving him his first look at his father.

Shock was too mild a word to describe his reaction. Spencer Campbell had always seemed strong and in control and…inviolable. He'd been the one constant in Mark's life during the turbulent period when everything else had fallen apart. Though Mark had never shared his grief over Bobby's death with his father, nor sought consolation from him when his mother died, he'd nevertheless counted on him to be there. His father's reliable, steady presence had helped him survive that devastating period.

But his father didn't look invincible now. His pallor was frightening and his face was gaunt, the familiar age lines transformed into deep grooves. None of his usual vigor was evident. Rick had said the stroke appeared to be mild, that there didn't seem to be cause for undue alarm. Mark wasn't sure he believed that.

Spencer's eyelids flickered open as Mark drew close, and when his clear gaze met his son's a smile lifted one corner of his mouth. "You look like you should be lying here instead of me. You must have been traveling all night. I told Rick not to bother you."

His voice was weak, his speech a bit slurred, but his

mind seemed sound, Mark noted with relief, trying to swallow past the lump in his throat as he reached for his father's hand. It had been years since he'd touched the older man—a fact that didn't escape his father's notice, judging by the flicker of surprise in his eyes.

"He would have been in big trouble if he hadn't."

"Sir, we need to take Mr. Campbell down for his scan."

As the nurse spoke behind him, Mark squeezed his father's hand. "They're going to do some more tests, Dad. Rick and I will be here when you get back."

"Why don't you two go home and get some rest? You know how hospitals are. This could take hours."

"We're not leaving."

"Hmph. You always did do things your own way. And that reminds me…I read that proposal you sent. Nice piece of work. We need to talk about it."

"Later."

"Count on it."

Mark stepped aside as they wheeled Spencer out. Rick was waiting when he exited the ICU.

"He said we should go home and get some rest," Mark relayed.

"Yeah, I know. He's been telling me that every ten minutes. Fat chance."

"Then he started to talk business."

Rick chuckled. "I'd say that's a good sign." Stifling a yawn, he consulted his watch. "I could use some food. Might help keep me awake. Besides, it's way past my breakfast time."

"I saw a cafeteria off the lobby."

"At this point, even hospital food sounds good. Let's go."

Ten minutes later, seated at a table tucked into a quiet corner, the two men dived into scrambled eggs and toast. Not until they'd taken the edge off their hunger did they resume their conversation.

"Is Allison okay?" Mark took a swig of his coffee, wishing he had some of the high-octane stuff from the *Gazette.*

"Yeah. I told her to stay home. She's about ready to pop, and stress is the last thing she needs. Besides, I didn't want Elizabeth hanging around here. This is no place for kids."

"Amen to that." The hours he'd spent in Bobby's sterile hospital room remained a vivid, unpleasant memory. "So tell me what happened with Dad."

"Not much to tell. The hospital called to let me know he was here. He sent for the ambulance himself. Until he was sure it was serious, he hadn't wanted to bother me, given Allison's condition. I plan to read him the riot act about that when he's back on his feet. Families are supposed to be there for each other—in bad times as well as good."

Tipping a little cream into his coffee, Mark watched the pale swirls seep into the dark liquid. "I haven't been very good on that score myself."

A few seconds passed while Rick took a measured sip of his coffee. "I figure there are reasons for that."

"Excuses, maybe."

"I like the word *reasons* better." Rick set his coffee down and regarded Mark without rancor. "Whatever the reasons you've distanced yourself from the family, I suspect they're powerful."

Struck by his brother's insight—and humbled by his nonjudgmental attitude—Mark was tempted to share those reasons with Rick. Yet he was afraid to open his heart. To make himself vulnerable. To take a risk.

Torn, Mark wrapped his hands around his cup. The cardboard flexed beneath his fingers, and all at once he was struck by the symbolism. The disposable cup reminded him of the way he'd lived for too many years. Use today, then throw it away. Don't expect permanence. Don't get attached to anything. Or anyone.

Over the past few weeks, Mark had begun to find that philosophy as flat and unappealing as the weak, tasteless brew from the hospital cafeteria. He'd resolved to try and turn things around. To make his life count for something. To tear down the wall around his heart.

He'd taken some tentative steps in that direction, but as his father's medical emergency had reminded him, he had no guarantee of unlimited time to rebuild the neglected relationships in his life. Perhaps this was his chance to start that repair work. And trust that God would give him the courage and strength to deal with whatever risks the task entailed.

"You're right," Mark conceded. "I did have reasons. But even I didn't understand them until the past few weeks." He dug deep for the courage to continue. "And the biggest one was fear."

Raising one brow, Rick assessed his brother. "You've never struck me as the kind of guy who's afraid of anything. You've always marched to the beat of your own drummer, did what you wanted, lived with gusto. Allison and I often talk about your glamorous life, all the fabulous trips and parties. I must admit that we experience momentary twinges of envy."

"Don't," Mark said flatly. "I'd trade it all in a heartbeat for what you have."

Shocked, Rick stared at him. "Are you serious?"

"Yeah." The comment had surprised Mark, too. Yet it was true, he realized, even if he hadn't put the thought into words until now. In the past few weeks he'd undergone a fundamental change. For the better. Rick and Allison had a strong, loving relationship and a wonderful daughter. They might not be able to match his lifestyle in a material sense, but what they had was far more valuable: a full, rich life in all the ways that counted. In contrast, Mark's existence seemed empty and bleak.

Tilting his head, Rick studied Mark. When he spoke, his tone was cautious. "You mentioned fear. I'm not sure I understand what you're afraid of."

"Letting people get close." Mark took a sip of the tepid coffee as he summoned up the courage to bare his soul. "Do you remember Bobby Mitchell?"

"Not too well. He was your age, and you guys didn't hang out with us kids. But I know you two were good friends."

"The best. Like brothers almost, from the time we were toddlers. When he died, part of me died, too. And when Mom died eight months later, I couldn't handle it. The thought of facing any more loss was too…terrifying."

His voice grew hoarse, and he stopped to clear his throat. "Anyway, after that I shut down. I decided that if I didn't let people get close, I couldn't get hurt. I felt the same way about God, since He'd let Bobby and Mom die. I was determined not to count on anyone or anything—including tomorrow. And that's how I've lived my life for more than twenty years."

"Wow." Several beats of silence ticked by while Rick digested Mark's revelation. "I had no idea you were hauling around all that heavy baggage. I think I can understand why you did what you did, but that's a lonely way to live."

"I know that now. And I'd like to change things. I want to reestablish my relationship with Dad. And with you. If it's not too late."

Rick's gaze never wavered. "It's not too late. And I know Dad feels the same way. Maybe that's one positive that will come out of this stroke. You'll be working more closely with him than ever while he recovers, so you'll have a great opportunity to reconnect. In fact, you might be taking over the helm of Campbell Publishing sooner than you anticipated, given Dad's condition."

Mark frowned and stared down at his coffee.

"For some reason, I'm getting the impression that you're not too thrilled about that," Rick ventured.

"I'm not."

"How come?"

"To be honest, the thought of running Campbell Publishing doesn't excite me."

"You're kidding!" Incredulous, Rick leaned forward. "You'll have the chance to shape the company for the future. To carry on the family tradition and add to

Campbell Publishing's record of honesty and truth in journalism."

"You sound like Abby." The flicker of a smile tugged at Mark's lips.

Puzzled, Rick shook his head. "Refresh my memory."

"The editor of the *Gazette,* where I've spent the past few weeks. She feels the same way you do about journalism and family tradition."

"And you don't." It was a statement now, not a question.

"I respect the family tradition. And I'd love to see it carried on. But I don't have the passion for journalism that Dad and Abby have. Or that *you* seem to have." A perplexed expression flitted across Mark's face. "You know, that's one thing I've never understood. Why didn't you join the firm when Dad asked you to after you finished college?"

His brother shifted, then focused on his empty coffee cup. "I hate to admit it, but to a large degree it was an ego thing. When I graduated, you'd just come on board. I could already see that Dad wanted to groom you to take over the lead spot. I don't know…I guess I wanted to make my own mark. And I knew I couldn't do that at Campbell Publishing. I'd always be in your shadow."

He looked back up. "But I'm not complaining, Mark. I like what I do. It's been a good and satisfying career. And I'm okay with the way things turned out."

"But I'm not." Frustrated, Mark raked his fingers through his hair.

"Have you told that to Dad?"

"No. I only came to that conclusion myself over the

past few weeks. When I stumbled onto a job that did excite me."

"Want to tell me about it?"

"Sure. Why not?" Mark took one last sip of coffee and set the cup aside. "While I was in Oak Hill, I got involved in coaching a boys' basketball team. When one of the promising players started slipping, I found out that his family was in the midst of a financial crisis. As I learned more I realized that there was a need to provide quick assistance to families facing unexpected and temporary crises."

His face grew more animated as he continued. "It kept eating at me, and then an idea stated to develop. For a charitable foundation that would serve the areas where Campbell Publishing distributes newspapers. The way I conceived it, boards of clergy would administer the program in our different geographic areas, all working through a central office here at headquarters. I researched other foundations, and put together a proposal for Dad to consider."

"I think that's a great idea!"

"Thanks." Mark flashed his brother a grin, encouraged by his enthusiasm. "Dad seems to think so, too. That's what he brought up as they were taking him away for his test a little while ago. He said he'd read the proposal, and he seemed receptive to the concept. I could really sink my teeth into a project like that, one that makes a tangible difference in people's lives and lets me use my finance background in a more humanitarian way. I'd love to direct the program."

Then Mark's grin faded. "But as you said, Dad's

always counted on me taking over. I can't see any way around that without disappointing him—and I've done that too often already in my life. Unless…" Suddenly his expression grew thoughtful.

"Unless what?"

"What about you? Would you consider it?"

"You mean…you're not talking about the CEO spot, are you?" Shock rippled across Rick's face.

"Why not? You're Dad's son, too. You're smart. You work hard. You have the right values. It's a perfect fit."

A flash of interest sparked in Rick's eyes before he managed to subdue it. "Except for two things. Dad might have other ideas. And I don't know the business."

"You could learn. We could work together until you felt comfortable. I don't think Dad's ready to turn over the helm yet, anyway, unless he's forced to for health reasons. But he seemed pretty alert to me a little while ago. There should be time for you to learn. And I doubt Dad would have any problem with the arrangement. You two have always gotten along."

"Let's not jump to any conclusions." Rick's voice was calm, but Mark picked up his undercurrent of excitement.

"Would you consider it?"

"I'd have to talk to Allison, of course. It would be a big change. But if she was okay with the idea…yeah, I'd give it some serious thought." Checking his watch, he wiped his mouth on a paper napkin and rose. "But this discussion may be premature. Why don't we table it until we get through Dad's crisis? I'm not sure any of us is thinking too clearly now. Ready to go back upstairs?"

"Sure." Mark stood, and as Rick started to turn away he placed a hand on his younger brother's arm. "And by the way…thanks."

"For what?"

"For making the effort to stay in touch all these years. For not resenting me because I was the 'heir apparent.' For being a great brother."

Rick's Adam's apple bobbed, and he shoved his hands into his pockets. "This is starting to sound mushy."

"Yeah. How about that?" With a grin, Mark gave him a playful shove and fell into step beside him as they headed for the elevator. "But you know what? It feels good."

As Abby pushed through the front door of the *Gazette* late Friday afternoon, Molly looked up. "Mark called while you were out. He said he'd try again later, but he wanted to let you know that his dad is doing better and that the stroke was mild. The doctors think his father will make a full recovery."

"That's good news. When did he call?"

"A little after one."

It figured. Abby had rushed back from St. Louis, hoping to hear from him. She was anxious to share Dr. Martin's assessment. An assessment Dr. Sullivan had seconded when she'd seen him earlier in the afternoon.

But perhaps it was best that she'd missed him. Since their conversation Monday night she'd been grappling with her own fears. And trying to come to grips with her situation. She no longer harbored any illusions about keeping the *Gazette* in the family. After reviewing the numbers again with Joe and the finance board this morning, it was clear they were operating on fumes. If Campbell Publishing didn't acquire the paper soon, it would go belly-up. Although turning her family legacy over to a conglomerate would be the hardest thing she'd ever done, watching the paper die would be worse.

At least Campbell Publishing seemed to be reputable, she consoled herself. Under Spencer Campbell's leadership, she expected that the *Gazette* would retain its integrity. It just wouldn't be hers anymore. And the notion of staying on as editor, which Spencer had suggested might be a stipulation of the sale, didn't appeal to her. At least not indefinitely. So what was she going to do with the rest of her life?

As she took her seat in her office, Abby ran a hand over the scarred desk, blinking back the sudden tears that sprang to her eyes.

Lord, I feel lost and confused. My whole world is being turned upside down. Please help me deal with my fears about the future...and about pursuing a relationship with Mark. And give me the courage to put my trust in You as I face decisions that will affect the rest of my life.

It had to be here somewhere.

Shoving aside another dusty box late Friday night, Mark gripped the edge of the final carton in the far corner of his guest room closet and pulled it out into the light. He'd promised Evan he'd look for his old astronomy book the next time he was in Chicago, the one with the amazing sky charts that he and Bobby had pored over for hours. They'd be outdated by now, but the main constellations hadn't moved. Evan would still be able to use the reference volume. Except it wasn't anywhere to be found.

It was possible that it had been given away, Mark conceded. After all, he hadn't seen the book in more than twenty years. But for some reason, he thought it was in one of the boxes he'd transferred from the closet in his boyhood room to this one when his father had sold the family home a couple of years back. He hadn't checked, though; he'd simply hauled the boxes over, unopened.

Dropping to one knee, he lifted the lid of the final box. A cloud of dust rose, and he sneezed several times. It would be easier to buy Evan a new book, he reflected. Why punish his sinuses? Yet the notion of passing on the book he and Bobby had prized to someone who shared his friend's passion for space appealed to him. Since he'd come this far, he might as well inspect the last box.

There were a lot of miscellaneous items in the carton, all dumped in haphazardly. Sifting through them, he found a realistic-looking plastic frog that had once sat on his nightstand—and had almost scared his mother to death when she'd first seen it, he recalled with a grin. A dog-eared comic book, a flattened Cubs cap, a miniature racing car—the items were all from the Bobby Mitchell era of his life. If he still had the book, it would be in this box.

Digging deeper, Mark's fingers closed around the spine of a bulky volume. Even before he pulled it free, the familiar feel of it in his hand confirmed that he'd hit pay dirt. Several other assorted objects were piled on top, and as he lifted the book out, he tilted it to let the odds and ends slide back into the box. But an envelope addressed to him caught his eye, and he grabbed for it as it started to slip away.

As Mark stared at the blue envelope, he set the astronomy book aside. He knew that handwriting. It was Bobby's. And all at once, a memory slammed into him, driving the breath from his lungs with the ruthless force of a mighty breaker crashing against jagged rocks.

It was the day of Bobby's funeral, and nothing anyone had said had been able to convince him to attend. Instead, he'd locked himself in his room, unable to accept the harsh reality of his friend's death. Even his mother's entreaties had fallen on deaf ears. In the end, his family had given up and gone without him.

Two hours later, when they'd returned, he'd still been in his room, still lying on his bed, still starting at the ceiling. His mother had come to his door, and her obvious worry had compelled him to respond so she'd at least know that he was alive. Once reassured, she'd slid the envelope he now held in his hands under the door. Her words came back to him as if she'd said them yesterday.

Mrs. Mitchell asked me to give you this, Mark. It's from Bobby. He wanted you to have it after...after he was gone.

For almost an hour Mark had stared at the blue rectangle lying on his beige carpet. Then he'd swung his legs to the floor, picked it up and shoved it deep into a box in the farthest, darkest, most hidden corner of his closet.

It had stayed there, forgotten, until now.

As Mark stared at the envelope, his hand began to tremble. How odd that after all these years, he would stumble on Bobby's card. A card containing a message that had never been delivered.

Bracing his back against the wall, Mark eased down until he was sitting on the floor. The seal was still tight on the flap, and after prying it open carefully, he withdrew the card.

The cover tightened his throat. It was so Bobby. Against an inky night sky filled with glittering stars, the Milky Way arched like a glowing celestial path to the heavens. A comet streaked across the infinite blackness, and in one corner a full moon, tinted pale blue, watched over the scene. Eight words overlaid the stars: *To my once-in-a-blue-moon friend.*

It took every ounce of his courage to open the card.

The printed message inside was simple. *Reach for the stars.* But it was Bobby's handwritten addition that gripped his heart—and wouldn't let go.

"I know we said we'd visit the stars together, Mark. But I guess I'm going first…in a way neither of us expected. I just wanted to tell you that you were the best friend I ever had. And that I know you're having a real hard time with this leukemia thing. It's a bummer, isn't it? But Father John was here yesterday, and he said I should tell you that even though God doesn't give us any guarantees about how long we're going to live, he does give us the ability to make every day count. And he gives us memory, so we can never really lose the people we care about.

"I feel like you and I did that, Mark. We made every day count. Please don't be sad when I'm gone, because I'll still be with you in all the memories we share. But if you start to miss me, look up at the sky and remember that the stars always shine—even when you can't see them. Just like love. Take care, buddy. Thanks for being my friend. And keep reaching for the stars!"

When Mark finished reading Bobby's message, he drew a long, shaky breath, leaned his head back against the wall and closed his eyes. He'd always known his friend was smart. He'd aced every test in school. But it seemed his heart had been as wise as his brain. At thirteen he'd understood more than Mark did at thirty-four.

Bobby had been right about guarantees, Mark acknowledged. No one was promised tomorrow. Nor was life's end necessarily precipitated by a warning. While he'd had notice of Bobby's impending death, he'd had none for his mother's. Life carried risk. So did love. Period. The only way to protect his heart from the risk of loss was to shore up the defenses he'd begun to dismantle over the past few weeks. As he'd begun to do with Abby when he'd realized that loving her was a risk. That there was no guarantee on her future. If he chose, he could continue down that path and return to the cold, sterile, empty existence that had been his life for the past twenty-one years.

But suddenly he realized that that was no longer an

option. For Bobby had been right about something else, too. As hard as it is to lose loved ones, the gift of memory allows them to live on in the hearts of those whose lives they touched. Though the loss of his mother and Bobby had been grievous, he wasn't sorry that either had been part of his life, for they had enriched it beyond measure. Just as Abby would if he gave her the chance, for however long he was blessed by her presence.

His throat constricted, and Mark looked down again at the card in his hands. Across the years, through time and space, Bobby's message still resonated. Perhaps even more now than when it had been written. And it had come to him when he had most needed to hear it. Now, as when they were young, Bobby's friendship had enriched his life. And he knew it always would.

A tear slipped out of Mark's eye and trailed down his cheek. Since the day Bobby died, he'd bottled up all his deeper emotions. Including grief. It had been safer that way.

But now it was time to release them. It was time to reach for the stars.

And for the first time in twenty-one years, he wept.

Chapter Sixteen

"Well, you boys look much improved today."

Rick and Mark exchanged smiles as they stepped into their father's room the next morning. After spending the day before at the hospital—and after being assured by the doctors that their father's stroke was, indeed, mild and that he would make a full recovery—they'd both headed home and crashed.

Only the rude beeping of his alarm clock had roused Mark at seven-thirty this morning. Forty-five minutes later, when Rick had swung by to pick him up, he'd still felt half-asleep. Rick hadn't seemed in much better shape.

Nevertheless, the two of them did look better than they had yesterday. As did Spencer. His color was back to normal, and he'd been moved to a regular room. The doctors had said that the minor lingering weakness in his left side would improve with time and therapy, as would the slight slur in his speech. He was doing so well, in fact, they expected to release him tomorrow.

All things considered, the Campbells had much to be

thankful for—as Mark had acknowledged to the Almighty this morning when he'd awakened.

"You're looking chipper yourself, Dad." Rick moved beside the bed and squeezed his father's hand.

"That's what I told the doctors. I'm not happy about spending the day flat on my back when there's work to be done at the office."

"It can wait," Mark told him. "Besides, it's Saturday."

"I'm not the type to lie around and do nothing," Spencer groused. Then he brightened. "I know—we'll talk about that proposal you sent. Sit down, sit down. You, too, Rick."

"Dad, I'm not sure the doctors want you to—"

"What they don't know can't hurt them," he countered, waving Rick's protest aside. "Besides, I'm going stir-crazy."

Mark angled a questioning look at Rick, who responded with a what-can-you-do? shrug. Capitulating, Mark perched on the windowsill on one side of the bed while Rick took a seat on the other side.

"Do you know anything about Mark's proposal?" Spencer asked Rick.

"He gave me the highlights yesterday."

"Good. That saves some time." Spencer turned his attention back to Mark. "It's a nice piece of work. Good research, excellent business case, sound philanthropic thinking. I like it. And it's a much more organized effort than anything we've ever done. The Bobby Mitchell Scholarship piece is a nice touch, too. A fitting tribute to a fine young man. So what prompted all this?"

Leave it to his father to cut to the heart of the matter, Mark thought. To want to know the whys as well as the hows. Condensing his experience with Evan and Reverend Andrews as much as possible, he briefed his father on the impetus for his idea.

When he finished, the older man gave an approving nod. "Sounds like your visit to Oak Hill has been productive on several fronts. How's your work on the *Gazette* going?"

"I just need a few more days to wrap things up."

"Give me the bottom line."

"The paper is well run, well respected and debt-free—but barely holding on by its fingernails. With the economies of scale we can bring to the operation, it should turn a nice profit."

Another satisfied nod from his father. "That's what I thought. I was very impressed with the operation. And the editor. Did you know that Pete Gleeson is thinking about retiring?"

The abrupt change of subject disconcerted Mark for a second. Pete was the editorial director for Campbell Publishing, but not someone Mark had much contact with. "No. Why?"

"It occurred to me that Abby Warner might be a good candidate for that job a few months down the road. After she assists with the *Gazette* transition and trains a new editor. Think she'd be interested?"

Stunned, Mark stared at his father. "I don't know. She's pretty devastated about losing the family legacy. And Oak Hill has always been her home." Still, if he could persuade her to move to Chicago, that would solve one of the major hurdles to their relationship, he realized. And if she became a Campbell, she'd be contributing to another, even larger family legacy. The possibility sent a current of excitement zipping through him, and he smiled. "But I like that idea."

"Why?" His father's blunt question, and the keen look in his eyes, brought a warm flush to Mark's neck. One that crept higher when he noticed Rick's speculative expression.

"Never mind," his father said with a chuckle. "I think I can figure it out. And by the way, I approve. Now, let's talk a little more about your proposal. We'll need a director. Have anybody in mind?"

The stroke might have slowed Spencer down physically, but Mark was having difficulty matching his mental agility. Folding his arms across his chest, he shot Rick a glance as he once more shifted gears. "I have a few thoughts."

"I figured you might."

Bracing himself, Mark plunged in. "Over the past few weeks, I've done a lot of soul-searching, and I've reconnected with a lot of things—including my faith. I've known for years that there was something missing in my life. A sense of purpose, for one thing. And I found it while I was in Oak Hill."

He took a steadying breath, summoning up the courage to continue. "The thing is, I feel the same excitement about this foundation that you do about the newspaper business, Dad. I'd like to direct the effort. I know you always expected me to take over when you retired, and I wish I had your passion for publishing. But the simple truth is, I don't. However, I found someone who does." He looked at his brother.

Spencer transferred his attention to Rick and gave him an appraising look. "Is that right, son?"

"Yes."

"All these years...you never said anything."

"He didn't want to live in my shadow." Both men turned back to Mark as he spoke. "He knew you had me pegged for the top spot. But he's the better man for the job."

Once more, Spencer looked at his younger son, his expression troubled. "I think I owe you an apology. When you turned down the chance to come on board after college, I didn't think you were interested in the family business. It appears I didn't look deep enough."

"It wasn't your fault, Dad. My own ego is what got in the way. I knew you'd welcome me to the company. But I also knew that Mark was being groomed for the CEO job, and I wanted to find a place where I could make a real difference."

"I can understand that," Spencer responded. "I felt the same way. That's why I started Campbell Publishing." He looked from one son to the other. "It seems you boys have this all worked out. And very well, I might add. I'm already feeling a bit superfluous." His tone was gruff, but the glint of humor in his eyes mitigated his words. As did his next comment. "But I expect I can still teach you both a thing or two."

"Or three," Rick acknowledged with a grin.

"At least," Mark affirmed.

"Well, I'd say we've already put in a good day's work. Now..." He turned back to his oldest son. "I think you have some unfinished business in Oak Hill."

"Yeah. There are one or two loose ends I need to tie up." A slow grin spread over Mark's face.

"Then get out of here. And tell Abby I said hello," he added, his eyes twinkling.

Abby broke off a bite of her peanut-butter cracker and popped it in her mouth. Her appetite had been nonexistent for the past couple of days as she'd tried to figure out what she was going to do with the rest of her life. But she had to eat. Her disease dictated it. Still, the crackers tasted as dry as cardboard, and she took a sip of water to try and wash them down.

Giving up the pretense of working, Abby leaned back in her chair and stared at the ceiling. In general, when she came into the office on a Saturday she accomplished a lot. Not today, however. Though she'd been here all afternoon—and part of the evening, she realized, checking her watch—the newspaper hadn't profited by her presence. But at least her thinking on two issues had clarified.

She was going to lose the *Gazette.*

And she loved Mark enough to at least test the waters of a relationship despite her fears about the pitfalls of trying to meld two divergent backgrounds.

That didn't mean she'd stopped worrying, however. While she didn't doubt the sincerity of Mark's interest, their connection would be harder to sustain over distance. Perhaps it would wane once they were separated. After all, their relationship was new, the strength of their feelings untested. She supposed he might suggest that she move to Chicago. But what if she agreed to do that, to disrupt her whole life, only to have the attraction fizzle in a couple of months?

There was also the question of how she would adjust to the big city if she did go. She was a small-town girl and Oak Hill was her home. The very notion of living in some high-rise condo downtown turned her off. Not that she could afford those kinds of digs, anyway.

A sudden click distracted Abby from her troubling thoughts, and she checked her watch again. Six forty-five. Harvey sometimes came in on Saturday to clean, but not at night.

Still wary from her recent hate-crimes experience, she rose and skirted her desk, keeping the hall in sight. As she reached her office door, a tall, dark-haired man came around the corner, and she froze. Mark!

He paused when he caught sight of her, and a slow smile lifted his lips and warmed his eyes, sending a crinkle of fine lines radiating from their corners. He was wearing jeans and a black leather jacket and his hair was windblown…and he looked so good, so appealing, that Abby had to muster every ounce of her self-control to keep from running down the hall and throwing herself into his arms.

But Mark seemed to have no such compunction. Dropping his overnight case, he covered the distance between them in several long strides and pulled her close, burying his face in her hair.

Wrapped in his embrace, his heart pounding steady and sure against her chest, Abby felt her tension dissolve. His ardent welcome chased away any fleeting wisps of doubt about the depth of his interest, dispelling them as surely as mist succumbs to the warmth of the sun.

At last, with obvious reluctance, he released her. Even then, he kept her safe in the circle of his arms, smiling down at her while his gaze caressed her face as if he was reacquainting himself with every nuance of her features. "I stopped by your house. When you weren't home, I figured you'd be here." He stroked a finger down her cheek. "I missed you."

"I missed you, too."

His smile deepened. "That's good to hear."

It was hard to be rational or practical when she was pressed this close to him, but Abby gave it her best shot. "How's your dad?"

"Much better. He should be going home tomorrow. He'll need some therapy, but the stroke was minor and there shouldn't be any lasting effects. In fact, he's back in fighting form already. He and my brother and I had an impromptu business meeting in his hospital room this morning. Some of it concerned you."

Surprised, she gave him a quizzical look. "You talked about me?"

"Uh-huh. And the *Gazette*."

A knot formed in her stomach. This was it. She'd known Mark was mere days away from finishing his review, and she was ninety-nine percent sure what his recommendation would be. While she'd tried to prepare herself for it, now that it was upon her, she didn't want to know. Dropping her chin, she made an effort to pull out of his embrace.

"Hey." He tightened his grip, forcing her to look back up at him. "It's not so bad."

She searched his tender, caring eyes. Eyes that said,

Trust me. And she wanted to. But no matter what he said, no matter how generous Campbell Publishing's offer was, the loss of the *Gazette* would be a failure she'd have to live with for the rest of her life.

Giving up the struggle to pull away, she rested in his arms, but her expression grew bleak. "You're going to buy the *Gazette,* aren't you?"

He could feel her trembling beneath his fingers. Moments before, he'd attributed her tremors to the emotion of their reunion. Now, he knew they were prompted by distress. And a sense of loss. He ached to pull her close again, to soothe away her fears.

But she needed more than whispered words of comfort. She needed something concrete to cling to that would bring the light back to her eyes and help her realize that she hadn't failed with the *Gazette.* He thought he could make that happen. He prayed he could. His own future, as well as hers, depended on it.

"Let's sit down for a few minutes. I have some things I need to tell you."

Draping an arm around her shoulders, he led the way back to her office. Since her desk took up most of the space, he propped one hip on the edge and entwined his fingers with hers as he surveyed the sturdy, battered oak surface. "I think this can hold us both. And I want you close."

In silence, Abby scooted beside him. And waited.

The ball was in his court. *Please, Lord, give me the words,* Mark prayed.

Taking a deep breath, he stroked his thumb over the back of her hand. "Do you remember when I came to

Oak Hill? How you thought I was a lazy, stuck-up playboy?"

Hot color suffused her cheeks. "I didn't—"

He pressed his fingers gently to her lips. "Yes, you did. And you were right. That was me for a lot of years. Too many. But after I came here I had some experiences that set me on a new path. I'm not the same man I was three months ago. And while a lot of people can claim a role in my transformation, you played the biggest one." He gave her hand a squeeze, then raised it to his lips and pressed a kiss to her palm before he continued.

"Let me skip all the whys and hows for now and cut to the bottom line. First, I realized that I don't want to be at the helm of Campbell Publishing. Instead, I want to create and direct a charitable foundation for the company that funnels our corporate donations directly to the grassroots level, to help families like the Langes that need immediate assistance. I put together a proposal for my father and he's endorsed the idea. My brother will join the firm to prep for the CEO position, in my place."

Her eyes widened. She opened her mouth to ask a question, but his next comment erased it from her mind.

"On a more personal level, I also realized that I need to take the padlock off my heart. I understand as well as anyone the risks of loving. But life without love is pretty empty. I know that firsthand, and I don't want to live that way anymore. That brings me to us."

He angled toward her and took her other hand in his. "I recognize that there are risks with diabetes. Perhaps more in your case, given your mother's history. But no one has a guarantee on tomorrow, Abby. I can't let what *might* happen stop me from pursuing what *can* happen. And as someone reminded me recently, we never really lose the people we care about. Even when they're gone, their love continues to shine in our lives—just as the stars do, though we can't always see them, either. I don't know how much time we'll be blessed with, but I'll treasure every day we have together. I love you, Abby. More than words can say."

His husky voice caught on the last word, and he cleared his throat. "You said once that if we ever got together, all the compromises would be on your side. That you were the one who would have to uproot yourself, leave the only home you've ever known. And you said you were afraid that you could end up resenting me, like your mother resented your father. I understand that concern. And I don't want that to happen any more than you do."

He lifted his hand and skimmed her cheek with the back of his fingers, his touch soft, his eyes earnest. "Abby, you of all people understand family legacies. I want to be part of Campbell Publishing—in a different capacity than originally intended but a vital one nonetheless. To do that, I need to live in Chicago. But I don't need the high-rise condo. I'm thinking more along the lines of a nice quiet suburb filled with big houses that have porch swings and white picket fences and flower gardens. And I also want to spend time in Oak Hill on a regular basis. This town will always be special to me."

His grip on her hands tightened, and she could feel the tremors in his strong fingers. "If you can live with all of that, I'd like to ask you to do me the honor of becoming my wife."

Abby stared up at him, her throat tightening with tenderness, and joy filled her soul with a radiant light, much as the fireworks had illuminated the night sky on the Fourth of July. She still didn't know what path God had in mind for her once her tenure at the *Gazette* ended, but she now knew that whatever direction her life took, Mark wanted to be by her side. Loving her with a depth that took her breath away.

And suddenly Abby also knew that if he could find the courage to get past his own formidable fears about her condition and offer her his love, she could find the courage to let go of the *Gazette* and find new work to give her life meaning.

A tear spilled out of her eye, and as it trailed down her cheek Mark released her hand long enough to wipe it away with a gentle, not-quite-steady finger. "This is too sudden, isn't it?"

"No." The word was barely audible and she tried again. "No, it's not. I feel the same way, Mark. I love you, too."

Relief refreshed his features as a sudden shower renews the earth after a long dry spell. "Does that mean you'll marry me?"

"Yes. I'm just trying to grasp the fact that despite the risks of my diabetes, you're willing to—"

He stopped her by once more pressing his fingers to her lips. "I've worked through that, Abby. I can live with the risks. Because I can't live without you."

No matter what gifts Mark might give her in the future, Abby knew that nothing would surpass this moment, when he'd given her his heart despite his background of loss, despite the years he'd been running from commitment, despite his fears that their marriage could be short-lived.

But now she had a gift for him in return.

Reaching up, she tugged his fingers aside. "You won't have to live without me, Mark. I have some good news. I talked to Dr. Martin. He researched my mother's files and there were no contributing factors to her death beyond negligence. He said there was no reason I shouldn't have a long life. Or a family of my own. I also saw Dr. Sullivan this week and he concurred."

As Abby watched, moisture clouded Mark's eyes. Then he pulled her close, clinging to her in a fierce hug that spoke of relief, joy, gratitude—and hope for all the tomorrows to come.

For a long time they held each other. But at last Abby eased back, far enough to look up at him. "How long can you stay?"

"A few days. I'm almost finished here. With business, at least."

A shadow passed across her eyes. They hadn't talked about the fate of the *Gazette,* and she didn't want to mar this moment. But it had to be faced. Yet, much as she dreaded the final pronouncement, she felt better equipped to deal with it now that she had Mark's love to sustain her.

"You're going to recommend the acquisition, aren't you?"

"Yes. Thanks to you—and your predecessors—the *Gazette* will be a tremendous asset for Campbell Publishing. Dad is very excited about it. But there's more."

He brushed a stray strand of hair back from her forehead, his fingers lingering on her satiny skin.

Clearing his throat, he let his hand fall back to her shoulder. "Anyway, Dad wants you to remain on board here and train a new editor for the next few months. But after that he'd like you to consider taking over as editorial director for all of the Campbell Publishing newspapers."

Stunned, Abby stared at Mark. "Are you serious?"

"Yes. He has great respect for your editorial integrity. Think of it this way, Abby—you could fight for truth in journalism on an even larger scale. Ensure that dozens of papers abide by the principles of honesty and integrity that have always been the hallmark of the *Gazette.* Your impact can be more far-reaching than that of any of your predecessors. This is your opportunity to take the Warner legacy to a new level."

Somewhere deep inside her the knot of tension that had been tightening for months began to uncoil. Could Mark be right? Was it possible that she hadn't failed after all? That her forefathers would be proud, not disappointed? After all, they had dreamed big, with broad vision. Maybe it was time she did the same.

As Abby looked at the man who had stolen her heart—and helped her find her future—she was filled with a joy unlike anything she'd ever experienced. Though she knew much change was ahead, she also knew that she had at last discovered God's plan for her. And with Mark by her side, with a dream to share, and with God's grace to guide her, she was ready to let go of the past and build a legacy of her own with the man she loved.

Mark watched as new warmth stole into the green eyes he had come to cherish. Watched as this special woman finally made peace with the future God had designed for her. For *them.* And when she reached out to him, he didn't hesitate. He folded her into his arms, where she belonged. Right beside his heart.

And as he bent to seal their promise to each other with a kiss, he thanked God. For the wisdom to leave yesterday behind. For the courage to open his heart to love. And for the chance to reach for the stars.

* * * * *

Dear Reader,

Welcome back to Oak Hill, Missouri, where romance blossoms again in the second of my three HEARTLAND HOMECOMING books. In *A Dream To Share,* Abby Warner wages the battle of her life as she fights to hold on to her family's publishing legacy. And Mark Campbell has a thing or two to learn about life—and love—as he descends from his big-city penthouse and plants his feet on solid ground.

As both Mark and Abby learn, God's will for us can often lead us in surprising—and sometimes scary—directions. But when we approach change with an open mind and heart, wonderful blessings can come our way.

Watch for Sheriff Dale Lewis's story, *Where Love Abides,* coming in May. To learn more about that book—and all my latest news—I invite you to visit my Web site at www.irenehannon.com.

May thoughts of spring brighten up the gray winter days still to come, and may your life always be blessed with the promise and hope of new beginnings.

Irene Hannon

QUESTIONS FOR DISCUSSION

1. In *A Dream To Share,* Abby believes she has failed to protect her family heritage. Have you ever been entrusted with an important task—and failed? How did you deal with it? What did you learn? How did your faith help you through the crisis?

2. Unlike Abby, who considers it an honor to carry on the family legacy, Mark regards it as a burden. Why? In light of his feelings, how might he have handled his situation differently? What impact would that have had on his life—and his brother's life?

3. Discuss Abby's work ethic and management style. What are the pros and cons of her passion for her work? What makes her a good people manager?

4. Abby seems to have accepted, and adapted to, her diabetes. Talk about chronic illness and how it can affect the life of the ill person and the lives of those who love him or her. What are some potential coping mechanisms? What role does faith play in dealing with illness?

5. The theme of prejudice is touched on in several places—the hate crimes, Mark's response to Abby's job-shadowing assignment and Mark's initial attitude toward small-town America. Too often, we

think of prejudice as simply a race issue. Talk about it in a broader context, and give some examples of prejudice you've observed or heard about. Why is prejudice wrong? What does the Bible teach us about prejudice?

6. Mark and his brother have never been close. Discuss the reasons why. Have any of these reasons affected your relationship with your own siblings? If so, what are some ways you might be able to overcome them?

7. As a child, Mark suffered the back-to-back losses of his best friend and mother, and those losses continue to influence his life. Do you have any childhood memories that still affect your life? In what way? If the impact is negative, what are some steps you could take to address them so they no longer have the power to hurt you?

8. What happened in Oak Hill to bring about the changes in Mark? Discuss specific examples and why they had an impact.

9. At one point, Mark asks Reverend Andrews, "Why does God let good people die so young?" Have you grappled with this question? What answers have you come up with?

10. Reverend Andrews also says that God sometimes leads us in surprising directions. Has He ever done that with

you? Describe your experience, as well as the challenges it brought and how you dealt with them.

11. Abby is convinced that dissimilar backgrounds in a marriage are a recipe for disaster, given the example of her parents. Do you agree? What are some problems that might result from such a match? How might those problems be addressed and overcome? Do you think Abby and Mark work out a satisfactory resolution in the end? Why or why not?

TITLES AVAILABLE NEXT MONTH

Don't miss these four stories in March

HEART'S HAVEN by Lois Richer
Pennies from Heaven

Cooking at the Haven, a new outreach mission in Chicago, was chef Cassidy Preston's way to pay back a huge favor. For Tyson St. John, the mission was a place to raise his nephew. Together they could make it their own haven as a family.

A TREASURE WORTH KEEPING by Kathryn Springer
Evie McBride planned a secluded summer running her dad's antique shop. But the teacher in her couldn't ignore a troubled teen who needed tutoring—or the teen's handsome uncle. Would this play-it-safe girl risk her heart for a treasure worth keeping?

MOUNTAIN SANCTUARY by Lenora Worth
Raising her son and running her B and B in rural Arkansas kept Stella Forsythe busy. She wasn't looking for romance until Adam Callahan came to town. The world-weary cop offered his services as a Good Samaritan. With a little prayer, he hoped they could find sanctuary in their budding love.

A SOLDIER'S FAMILY by Cheryl Wyatt
Wings of Refuge

Pararescue jumper Manny Pena had stuck his foot in his mouth when he'd met Celia Munoz. Now he was desperate to make amends. But Celia wasn't having it. Could his growing commitment to her and her troubled son begin to convince her that perhaps she should take her own leap of faith?